An Act of God

Dedication

To:
D.R.H.

An Act of God

Lloyd Hornbostel

1996
Galde Press, Inc.
Lakeville, Minnesota

An Act of God
© Copyright 1996 by Lloyd Hornbostel.
All rights reserved.
Printed in the United States of America.
No part of this book may be used or reproduced in any manner whatsoever without written permission from the publishers except in the case of brief quotations embodied in critical articles and reviews.

First Edition
First Printing, 1996

ISBN 1–880090–33–3

Galde Press, Inc.
PO Box 460
Lakeville, Minnesota 55044

Contents

Chapter 1	Malfunction	1
Chapter 2	Confirmation	7
Chapter 3	Classified	17
Chapter 4	Presentation	29
Chapter 5	Coverup	35
Chapter 6	Escape	47
Chapter 7	Fugitive	57
Chapter 8	Exposé	67
Chapter 9	Refuge	77
Chapter 10	Ice	87
Chapter 11	Critique	97
Chapter 12	Panic	107
Chapter 13	Sinking	117
Chapter 14	Evacuation	125
Chapter 15	Slide	137
Chapter 16	Reunion	145
Chapter 17	Contact	155
Chapter 18	Home	167
Chapter 19	Coming	177

Other Books by Lloyd Hornbostel

War Kids 1941–1945: WW II Through the Eyes of Children
 (Galde Press, 1996)

1. Malfunction

"Telephone, Warren"—Sally's voice carried out over the patio. Oh no. He knew the meaning of a weekend call—trouble at the center. Warren Belting put down his cup of coffee and the Saturday paper, got up, and came into the house. Sally handed him the phone.

It was Lynn at control. "We've got something wrong with Solar III. You'd better come over for the next check run." Warren muttered a few remarks about the solar project in general, and hung up. He was in charge of all operations at Houston base—admittedly a good job, and with a salary far in excess of any comparable civilian technical job he had ever held in the past. The worst part of the position was the phone calls—somehow equipment always failed on weekends. There must be a law, he thought, as he exchanged his swim trunks for the base uniform. Warren grabbed his manuals and went to find Sally.

Sally had been busy with preparations for their couple's club dinner, and he knew that she would probably be "solo" again. The club meant a great deal to Sally, and she wouldn't be pleased to see the base uniform. She wasn't. "I suppose you'll spend the night at operations," she said, answering her own question.

Warren gave the usual shrug of the shoulders and replied, "It's Solar III. I'll have to wait out the next check run before I can tell anything." The truth was that this was all he did know—though Sally never quite believed him.

She always felt that the base was secret, and her not being allowed entrance to operations did not help matters. Warren could of course only discuss the various projects in general terms because most of the work was classified in nature.

"Give my regrets to the crew," Warren called from the garage as the pickup roared into life. There was no answer from the house, and he started the forty-five-minute run to the base mulling over the history of Solar III.

Solar III was a joint government-university research effort culminating in an orbital satellite designed to return data to earth concerning the sun's energy output. The whole project had been a mess as far as Warren was concerned; fighting among the university professors coupled with their almost total lack of understanding concerning technical function had made Warren's task difficult. And now, after only ten days in orbit around the sun—malfunction.

"Dammit to hell, anyway," Warren thought as the pickup truck nosed through the Saturday traffic. "All those lucky bastards going out for Saturday night."

He knew that his chances of joining Sally were slim because the checkout alone could run several hours before any attempt at correcting the malfunction would be possible.

Lynn, as usual, had not given any details—she'd make a good spy, Warren mused as he swung into the security point. He flashed his ID, and the guard nodded him through.

Lynn was waiting for him at building 1077, along with several of the university's "brain mob," as Warren called them.

"Dammit," he thought, "I'll have to explain every move twice." There was no other way—they had paid for half the project, and seemed to have nothing else to do but ask stupid questions.

"Hi Lynn, what's up?" Warren felt better at seeing one friend. Lynn was his secretary, assistant, general hand, and counsel. She made work bearable, and at times almost pleasant, particularly in the case of Solar III.

"It's going to be a long night," Lynn commented. "The profs are fighting over the data."

Warren entered the main control center where a group of people were clustered around one of the monitors. As Warren approached, they parted to allow him to check the monitor screen. The data was coming in and Warren first checked background, followed by sequencing the various scans. As far as he could determine, all was in order.

As if in answer to his question, Professor Fellstrom, who was in charge of the university team, stepped forward and spouted: "It's not right; the data is all wrong." Warren started to mutter a word in his defense, but was stopped by a printout sheet thrust in his hand. "Look, these figures are impossible." The professor was both excited and ornery. His hand pointed to a line of numbers on the sheet. "The therms are dropping! Everything is dropping."

Gradually, Warren began to understand. The data was coming through properly, but low, too low to be correct. Something must have gone wrong with the main power supply, or computer. He had an elaborate system checkout program, one that would require several hours of work to complete, but it was the only thing left to do. Lynn had done her usual fine job of going through the corrections, and all were positive. He called Lynn aside: "All we can do is run a complete system c.o.; can you stay and help?" He knew she would—it was only a courtesy to ask her.

She smiled, "I'll start right away." Warren called Professor Fellstrom aside and explained the procedure. He also advised him that it would probably be midnight before anything definitive would be available. Professor Fellstrom muttered something about supper, and a possible return to the center, but Warren knew from past experience that he would not see any more of the university team until Monday morning.

It was past 9:00 P.M. before Warren and Lynn finished setting up the checkout program. Essentially each experiment aboard Solar III would be double-checked by two independent systems. Warren had developed the procedure, and had "salvaged" a number of otherwise useless satellites. Perhaps, he thought, Solar III would be another success to add to his list.

The total transmission time took forty-five minutes, and the last printout was finally displayed on the screen. Now for the comparisons, thought Warren. His mind was that of a technical professional; he placed ultimate faith in his equipment, and was seldom disappointed. Lynn, on the other hand, needed a certain amount of personal assurance. She enjoyed Warren's technical competence, but often wished he could communicate somewhat more personally. Tonight though, the two of them were intent on one mission—the salvage of Solar III.

The two columns of data started to appear on the screen. After only a few minutes the obvious was apparent—both columns were identical, and reading low, much, much too low to be of any value. Warren and Lynn were both disappointed. Not so much from the lack of data, but because of their inability to correct the system.

"Fifteen million bucks worth of junk," commented Lynn. She switched off the monitor and started the task of filing the printout sheets. "The ol' prof and his crew will love us," she said, but she really didn't care.

Midnight was approaching when the two had completed the shutdown. Warren had written off the club party and would face Sally's wrath later. His disappointment was total. "Let's grab something to eat and get out of here." Lynn felt some food and drink would cheer both of them, and provide some time to rethink the mission. No thought of supper had entered anyone's mind during the effort to correct the malfunction.

Harry's Steak House was a place most people would pass by. Totally lacking any exterior paint or interior decor, its owner concentrated on serving "the best steaks in Texas," a boast proudly proclaimed by a weathered sign over the bar. Lynn and Warren found a table in the corner and were immediately recognized by the owner, Harry Ross.

"You two look like you lost your best friend!"—Harry could read faces—"First round is on me." Life always looks better after food and drink, and the two found themselves trying to rationally critique the mission. The answer was always the same—a major malfunction unknown to either of them. Their thoughts were interrupted by Harry's bar bell, a relic from his war years aboard an aircraft carrier. "G'night folks. Y'all come back and see us." The "us" was an unknown; save for an aged Oriental dishwasher, Harry ran everything by himself.

"I'll run you home," Warren offered, as was his usual custom when they worked late. Houston was safe enough, but 2:00 A.M. is a questionable hour in any city. The old pickup responded to the key, and Harry's was left for another time.

Lynn lived alone as far as Warren knew. She had an older brother in the priesthood, but no other relatives. A single light glowed from the porch of a house with more past than future. Lynn touched him on the hand, "Good night, War," paused for an instant, and disappeared behind the glow.

Warren somehow felt there was more to their relationship, but beyond a strange feeling when she touched him, nothing became of it. He pushed the pickup home to Sally, who he hoped would be asleep and not want an instant replay of the evening's events. He left the pickup in the drive so he wouldn't disturb her by opening the garage door, walked into the living room, and collapsed on the sofa.

2. Confirmation

Sometime during the night Warren awakened with a cold chill. As often, his mind was still at work on the project. The thought that occurred to him was simple enough. What if the satellite were fully operational? All of the tests conducted thus far had assumed that Solar III was malfunctioning, and that the data was in error. If in fact all was operational then some strange, unknown force could be cutting the sun's energy output. Perhaps in his disappointment Warren was reaching too far for answers, and yet no proof existed for the malfunction.

Warren could not get back to sleep. His mind refused to give in to reality. *Dammit.* Warren got up off the sofa and went out to the pool patio. *Maybe I can get some sleep out here in the fresh air,* he thought. He found a reclining chair and lay down, his mind still much too active for sleep. Strange, now his thoughts were of himself and Sally. They had met at a base party in Melbourne, Florida, during the peak boom days of the space program. Sally then as now was a professional model; she was quite a catch for an Iowa farm boy fresh out of school. They had never had any children, something which bothered Warren. Sally had wished to continue her modeling career, and pregnancy had no place in her life. Now after almost twelve years and two moves later, it seemed as if the child-rearing years had passed them by. Warren missed the activity of a family; he had been one of nine children on a farm, but in many respects his job consumed his needs. He had accomplished much professionally, rising from a laboratory position to staff, and now was in charge of the Houston Center Operations.

The sun rising in the morning sky brought Warren back to the present; he rose, tired, from the chair and made his way to the kitchen, hoping that some breakfast would revive him. Making his own breakfast was nothing new, because Sally always slept late. Dinner was their only meal together. Eggs, toast, bacon, and coffee brought him around to the realities of Sunday at home. Warren decided to say as little as possible about the events of the evening to Sally. It would avoid arguments, and he was not sure in his own mind exactly what had occurred. He would discuss his theory with Lynn Monday morning prior to his dreaded session with the university team. Professor Fellstrom's reaction would be predictably ugly, and the less said the better.

"Warren, have you picked up the paper yet?" Sally always liked her coffee and paper in their bedroom on Sunday. Warren's preoccupation with the satellite made him forget his usual routine.

"Coffee's hot, I'll be right in," he called. Gathering the paper and a tray with the coffee he made his way to their room.

"Where were you?" Sally had obviously rankled over his absence last night and was letting him know it.

"I didn't get home 'til almost three, honey. We had a real go at Solar III." He hoped this would end the discussion, and for once it did. Sally was cool toward him the remainder of the day, but Warren felt it a blessing. He spent his day trying to piece together a logical report for the university team and a rational critique for Lynn.

Monday morning Lynn met Warren at security. She too had spent considerable time reviewing the events of Saturday. She was not willing to concede defeat, but, she had not come up with any other theory as Warren had.

"Lynn, don't think I'm nuts, but I've got to tell you my idea before this whole thing drives me crazy." He then told Lynn his theory, watching her carefully during his discussion.

She made no comment until he had finished, then, "I'm scared, War. I hope that you're wrong, but I don't know." Lynn's education had included enough social and natural science to make her realize the worldwide implications of a cooling climate. Warren had not thought of this aspect of his theory, but he began to understand.

"If we even mention it to the prof, he'll go bananas," Warren answered, knowing Lynn's thoughts.

"What are we going to use for the critique?" Lynn asked. Warren would have to be in charge of the presentation, and he honestly was at a loss for words. He had two options. Either scrub the mission, or fabricate some story. Warren's basic integrity, and technical competence, ruled out the latter option.

"Let's talk to Charlie." Lynn, as often the case, came up with another out.

C. A. "Charlie" Richardson was in charge of all Houston Operations. He combined the talents of a Marine bird colonel and physicist to perfection. His time was not to be wasted, but both Warren and Lynn felt his counsel would be valuable. If Warren's theory had any validity, Charlie would know how to deal with it. There would be another system check at 11:00 A.M., and the proposal was to have Charlie at the monitor. Professor Fellstrom and his crew would be given an early lunch, and hopefully Warren, Lynn, and Richardson could conclude on a reasonable course of action.

Lynn and Warren got the data together, and Warren made up a graph of the energy figures taken each day. The line connecting the points definitely showed a decrease in output, a trend that would soon be felt on the earth's surface if it continued. He had coined a name for the theory—"Solar Dimming"—and as he worked on the presentation, the theory seemed to sound more like fact.

"I got Charlie for ten-thirty," Lynn called from the office. "Did you tell him anything?" Warren was worried Charlie might throw the whole thing out.

"Only that Solar III had a major problem and we wanted to clear our conclusion with him." Lynn knew Charlie better than Warren did because she had been his secretary prior to working with Warren, and she respected Charlie.

Charlie Richardson's office was warm, comfortable, and filled with the mementos of thirty years of military and civilian service to his country. He was the link between the Houston operations and Washington; a vital link when politics and the budget were concerned. Policy was something Warren and Lynn had never had to consider; until now they had been totally insulated from such matters.

"Come in! Nice to see you two." Charlie made everyone feel at home. "Solar III acting up again, eh? Wish we could get rid of that whole mess."

Charlie had never been sold on these joint projects; his military mind knew of the communications problem, and he had done a stint teaching at a Midwestern university, making him familiar with handling professors. Nonetheless he had hoped that the public relations aspect of the project would be worth the effort.

Warren briefed Charlie on the project up to the Saturday incident, and then recapped their critique, being careful not to place any extra emphasis on the solar dimming theory. He explained the graphs along with a brief summary of his own thoughts on the matter.

Warren was about to finish when Lynn interrupted. "It's almost eleven; let's check the monitor.

The data was coming in when the three of them arrived. Warren had added a scan program so that the earlier data could be compared directly on the screen. The trend was the same, only now the energy levels were even lower—the rate of change was increasing. Charlie watched the monitor for about ten minutes without saying a word, something quite unusual for Charlie. When he turned to Warren and Lynn his face was drawn.

"We'd better go back to my office."

Charlie was straight and to the point. "I don't know what in the hell is going on up there, but none of this gets beyond this office. Do you understand?" Warren and Lynn nodded, more of a reflex reaction; they had never seen Charlie this way. "Warren, if your theory, 'solar dimming' I think you called it, is correct, how much time do we have until we have a reaction on earth?"

Warren was taken by surprise! He had never thought of such direct consequence; "I don't know, possibly two or three weeks, maybe less if one had the proper instruments for measurement."

Charlie then asked the key question: "Do you still think that we have a malfunction?"

Warren and Lynn both shook their heads, negative. For a few moments C. A. Richardson's office was quiet, save for the ticking of a desk clock; somehow the passage of time began to take on new meaning to the three figures locked in silence. Charlie broke the silence.

"Those profs, get rid of them, tell them we have a possible malfunction, and it will take a few days to clear it. I'll classify the project secret to keep them out." (They were short, clear orders.) Charlie's military mind was working. "As for you two, no word to anyone." The fact that he had repeated himself made Warren and Lynn aware of the importance of the order. "I'm going up with this, I'll need a couple of days."

"Going up" meant only one thing—Washington D.C.; it was clear that Charlie was worried, and like Warren and Lynn, a little scared.

Charlie rose slowly from his chair and walked across the room to the full glass window. Looking up at the sun, he whispered under his breath, "You bastard, you'd better keep shining."

It was his signal to leave, so Warren and Lynn quietly made their exit. They had their orders.

"Those profs will be back from lunch now. We'd better start with them." Warren wanted to get the confrontation over with as soon as possible. His critique was more of an excuse than a lie; at least the possibility of a malfunction still existed. His next problem was Sally; he'd work that one over on the way home.

The university team assembled, quietly, in the conference room as if they knew bad news was forthcoming. Warren was to the point.

"Gentlemen, as you know we have had some trouble with Solar III. I don't have any idea how long it will take for corrective action, but we feel that it will be at least several days. You will be advised when we are back on target. That's all."

They were neither happy nor satisfied, but he left them with no options. Professor Fellstrom asked the only question, "Is that all?"

Warren replied firmly, "Yes." He could not tell if any of them were suspicious, but Warren knew any further discussion would cause nothing but harm. With a "thank you, gentlemen," he closed the session.

Lynn spent the remainder of the afternoon getting the critique reports ready for distribution. From the contents, one had no idea of the real problem. *Well,* she thought, *Charlie had asked for a malfunction, and he got one!*

Warren went back to the Solar III monitor to view the afternoon's data transmissions. Since Charlie had already classified the area, he was alone. As he viewed the data, showing the ever diminishing solar energy levels, Warren began to realize the fuller implications Charlie had mentioned earlier that day. A cooler earth would mean little or no food and eventual world starvation. His mind envisioned a world covered with ice; the vision had already taken some aspects of grim reality. With energy levels dropping as they seemed to be on the monitor, it would be only a matter of years—or months.

"Can you give me a ride home?" Lynn's voice interrupted Warren's thoughts—the day had passed in one hell of a hurry.

"Sure, if you don't mind the truck." She never seemed to complain, but he felt almost apologetic about the condition of the vehicle. One of these days he must find time to rebuild it.

They were both quiet on the way to Lynn's apartment; the events of the day were too heavy on their minds for idle conversation. The truck turned into the drive and groaned to a stop; the brakes also needed attention. Lynn was the first to speak.

"I'd be happy to fix a snack for you." She knew that Sally's TV modeling job would mean Warren's eating alone. Lynn also had a selfish motive; she wanted to be with Warren and not spend her evening alone.

"We'd best not hit Harry's tonight; the university team might be drowning their sorrows and the last thing we need is to run into them after that critique!" It was more of an excuse for Warren than a reality; the team was probably homeward bound on a jet.

Warren needed little coaxing; he was both hungry and tired, and Lynn's cooking could be no worse than a thawed TV dinner.

"Fine." He got out and helped Lynn out of the cab.

Warren had never been inside Lynn's apartment; their relationship consisted of working together and an occasional ride home. Tonight they shared a potentially awesome secret made worse by their inability to discuss it with anyone except each other.

Lynn unlocked the door. "What do you think of it?" He found himself in the center of a bright studio apartment, walls lined with books, and plants growing everywhere. The room was neat, orderly and yet full of just enough clutter to make it livable.

"Beautiful," was all Warren could say, as he flopped on the couch.

"Like a drink? Might not be as good as Harry's, but I'll try." Lynn opened a cupboard in the kitchen and the rattle of ice cubes brought Warren around.

"Scotch on the rocks, and make it strong." Lynn returned with his request, plus her usual gin and tonic.

"I've got a couple small steaks and salad materials. Will that do?"

"Fine, great," Warren gave his Scotch a long draw; the day gained a little perspective. He turned and studied Lynn beside him on the couch. She was trim; she always wore rather plain blouse and skirt combinations, and her auburn hair up in a twist, secured with a leather clasp. Lynn was quietly pretty, and always had a kind twinkle in her eye. He wondered why she had never married.

"Feel better?" She had been studying him, almost without his knowing it. God, what would Sally say if she knew his whereabouts!

"Yeah, much. I wonder how Charlie will do in D.C. We gave him one hell of a mission."

Lynn looked him in the eye with a quiet gaze. "What do you think, War?"

"I'm sure we have no malfunction—there's just no way all those systems could reproduce that kind of data. I don't know enough about the sun's output to guess what's going on. Sure wish I could have leveled a little more with the profs."

He then told Lynn of his thoughts that afternoon; the more he talked, the more he became concerned about the repercussions on earth.

"Where will we live? How will we eat? I wish to hell somebody else had Solar III."

"Let's eat." Lynn got up and moved to the kitchen. He watched her. Lynn the assistant was now Lynn the woman. *I'd better slow down on this Scotch,* Warren thought to himself. He couldn't take his eyes off her as Lynn moved about the tiny kitchen; his mind envisioned her as some slow, exotic dancer. *Damn.* He got up and went over to the bookcase. It didn't work; he found himself back in the kitchen.

"May I do something?" Lynn turned, handed him the plates and silverware, then gave him a smile that almost made him drop them. Perhaps if he concentrated on setting the table. She passed him the salad.

"I'm almost ready; there's a bottle of red wine in the 'fridge. Could you get it opened?" All he needed, he thought: Scotch, topped off with wine on an empty stomach.

The meal was quiet. Warren thought of his first dinner date; he was so scared he couldn't speak. Lynn interrupted his thoughts.

"What will it be like here—I mean, on earth, if it keeps up, will we freeze or something?"

"Ski sales should be brisk here." Warren was trying to be funny, only it didn't come out funny. "I'm sorry Lynn. I guess I'd rather not think that far ahead. I suppose we'd better hope Charlie convinces D.C. to make preparations." As soon as he said the words he felt the stupidity of the whole matter; how do you prepare for an ice age? "Can I help you clean up?"

"No thanks, just relax, there isn't that much," he moved to the couch, half asleep with the combination of food and liquor. *Who was that ancient goddess who drugged her suitors?* he wondered.

He awoke to find his head in Lynn's lap. She was smiling at him. "Feel better?" That was just the damn problem: he'd never felt better. He placed his hand on hers. She smiled that kind, quiet smile, and he was asleep.

Warren awoke with a start: the room was light—the *sun* was up! "Oh my God!" Lynn had removed his shirt, trousers, and shoes and covered him with a blanket. He half stumbled around the room.

"Lynn!" He was frantic.

"Hi." Lynn emerged from the bedroom, dressed in an all-too-revealing night dress—not bad.

Panic hit Warren. "I've got to get home! Sal will kill me."

"I'm sorry to report that you were a perfect gentleman." She smiled as Warren made a heroic effort to dress. Somehow he found the front door.

"See you at the lab," she called, as Warren regained enough composure to start the truck. As he lurched down the street, his watch told him he would see Lynn at the lab, and soon. There was no time to drive home.

3.
Classified

C. A. Richardson was in his office earlier than usual. He had to call D.C., and the time difference would mean that a 7:00 A.M. call might just catch Gus before he started his daily meeting schedule. Dr. Gustav Olsson was in command of all domestic scientific operations. He delegated project responsibility and budget allocations. He was, among other things, Charlie's boss. Gus too had a military background, dating back to the WW II Norwegian resistance movement. His specialty had been rocket propellants. Gus was one of the few men outside Nazi Germany to know detailed information concerning the V2 German rocket. He had joined the Allied effort, first in England and then in the U.S. Gus looked the classic Viking, tall, blond, with deep-set blue eyes. He could out ski and out swim men half his age.

"Hi, Charlie, how's Texas?" boomed Gus's voice over the phone.

"Hot and stinking." Charlie had yet to become used to the Houston summers. "I hate to bother you about this, but we have had some unusual reception from Solar III. Down here we feel that we're monitoring a rapid decrease in energy output. As to the cause, I'd say our opinion is that Solar III is fully operational; it must originate from some solar disturbance."

Gus was silent for a moment then asked, "How long has it been going on?"

"We don't know exactly," replied Charlie. "We caught it on the monitor last Saturday and went through the full malfunction checkout Sunday. I got the university group out of here yesterday as a precaution—they think we've got a mechanical."

He was worried Gus would not understand his concern. He just had so little to go on at this point. Gus interrupted his thoughts.

"Have you got printouts?"

"Yeah, we got all of them." Warren, he hoped, had kept everything.

"Send it up, classified and muzzle that project. I'll call you tomorrow, and Charlie, thanks for keeping me covered."

Charlie felt relieved, "Thanks, Gus. I'll copy."

Charlie leaned back in his chair and thought for a moment. Gustav Olsson was a man of secrets. He never told you his exact impressions. Well, at least he wasn't disturbed with the interruption. Charlie pushed his call button: "Get me Warren Belting."

Warren heard the call in the locker room where he was in the process of repairing last night's damage. Fortunately, he had a clean shirt and tie in the locker; a shower and shave had done the rest. Warren dialed Charlie's code; his secretary answered.

"Mr. Richardson wants all the data on Solar III, code classified, sent to Dr. Olsson. He said you'd understand."

"I'll have it out by noon." Warren headed for the monitor, then stopped in the hall; he'd better call Sally. He decided simply to tell her that Solar III had been classified, that part was true, and he'd had to spend the night working (not true).

"Hello, Sal, Warren, yeah, the first time I've had a chance—"

That was as far as he got before Sally came through loud and clear: "Where in the hell have you been? I had cold chicken at eleven last night. I'm going to reheat yours tonight, and you damn well better be here."

He heard the phone slam as she terminated the conversation. Well, at least he had some time to think of a better story.

The Center had a direct phone connection with D.C. All transmissions were automatically coded, if required, and transmitted in a matter of seconds, then decoded at the other end. He was almost finished with the input when Lynn caught up with him.

"Have a nice sleep?" She was obviously in good humor.

"One more comment and I'll let you talk to Sally." He didn't mean it, but his perspective on last night's events was limited.

Lynn changed the subject. "What are you doing?"

"Charlie wants all we have on Solar III sent to D.C. He must have talked to Gus this morning. Must be important, because he asked for code. I'll keep sending as we receive from the monitor." Warren concluded his task and got up, slowly.

"You need some coffee; let's get some," Lynn said, and she was right. He was about ready to fall asleep.

In Washington, Gustav Olsson watched the data sent from Houston as it was decoded and displayed in his reviewing room. He was alone. Gus had the mind of a sleuth, honed keen during his years in the underground movement. It was his special ability to connect seemingly unrelated events into a logical pattern that would define the appropriate action. Something else had a parallel to Solar III. He called his secretary.

"Don't make any printouts of this data—it's classified. Also could you get me last week's project summaries, please?" She nodded, and returned to her office.

Dr. Olsson required a weekly review of all joint scientific projects; this minimized communications problems and made all researchers aware that continued financing of any program was based on results. Something in one of the reviews, he was not certain which one, reminded him of Charlie's phone call.

"Here are the reports, Dr. Olsson." His secretary left a substantial stack of papers on his desk.

"Thanks, and don't disturb me for an hour or so."

It was midmorning when Gus found what he was searching for—the Wilson Antarctic file. Ken Wilson, a young man working on his Ph.D. in physics, had devised a method to measure freezing and thawing cycles and had been funded to experiment in the Antarctic. His device was simple, yet effective: a solution of distilled water and antifreeze with a known freezing point was contained in a vial with a movable lid. Freezing of the solution raised the lid due to the ice expanding and closed an electric switch. Each unit was connected to a radio transmitter, and when freezing occurred, a signal was sent to a central station. It was hoped that the information gained would provide an indication of the Antarctic climate's effect on the glacier.

One sentence in the last report caught Gustav Olsson's eye: "All stations freezing, have added 2% E.G. (ethylene glycol) to solution, but freezing continues. Cannot explain."

How many times, he mused, had seemingly unrelated incidents been connected to gain intelligence information. The war years in Norway were like that. Was he looking at two pieces of information telling a common story? It was little to go on, but all he had at this moment.

Gus had two choices: he could launch a massive investigation to confirm one way or the other if a solar disturbance was cooling earth, or he could make a judgment based on the facts before him. His intelligence experience made Gus aware of possible security complications; other countries might be aware shortly of the problem. Involving too many people would make keeping the theory secret extremely difficult. Through his experience during the war he had learned the need to control information. Gus decided on the route of caution.

Two calls were dispatched from the office of Dr. Olsson that morning: one to C. A. Richardson, Houston, Texas, and one to K. A. Wilson, McMurdo Sound, the Antarctic. Both messages were the same: Classified conference, Washington D.C. Friday, 10:00 hours. That gave all parties exactly two days.

Warren picked up the phone. It was Charlie's secretary.

"Mr. Richardson would like to see you."

"Okay, I'm on my way."

He met Lynn at the elevator. She asked, "You get a call from Charlie?"

"Yeah," Warren replied, "I guess he got through to D.C." He wondered if Charlie had communicated directly with Dr. Olsson, and what had transpired. Well, they'd soon know.

"Come on in." Charlie's office door was open. "Please be seated, and, Warren, close the door." Charlie wasted no time. "I've talked to Dr. Olsson this morning, and this just came in." He showed them the D.C. meeting notice. "I can't give you any more information now, but transportation will be arranged, I'm sure. One thing though, Dr. Olsson wants all Solar III activity classified. I have no formal orders, but I'm sure you understand."

Warren and Lynn understood well enough; Charlie had made an impression on Dr. Olsson and the urgency of the reply made them all nervous.

"Oh, Warren, keep updates coming on the monitor. I'm sending everything to D.C."

Charlie got up and walked to the door. He opened it slowly and turned to his guests. "Security is damn important," he said.

Warren and Lynn returned to his office after the brief session with Charlie. Lynn was the first to speak.

"He looked worried—and sorta tired."

Warren nodded. "I know. There's nothing we can do, though, till the D.C. meeting. We better get everything on Solar III in some reasonable order; that Dr. Olsson is a heavy."

"Let's go out for lunch," Lynn said. "I need to get away from here."

"Fine," Warren felt the same way. "I'll see you in the parking lot at twelve."

Charlie's classified order had one positive effect, Warren decided as he dialed home. He could not possibly tell Sally about last night's events without detailing Solar III. It was a coward's way out, he admitted to himself.

"Hi Sal, Warren." Silence on the other end. "We have been classified, and honest, honey, I can't say anymore."

"My, you come up with some dandies—classified! I'll *bet* last night was classified. You damn well better be here tonight!"

Warren was relieved as she clicked off; tonight would not be any honeymoon, but at least Sally was talking. He'd have to tell her about the D.C. trip, but he decided to avoid mentioning Lynn's participation. Technicians are almost never involved in high-level meetings, so Sally, he hoped, would not ask the question. Warren looked at his watch; it was almost twelve noon.

"What are these meetings like?" Lynn asked as they left the base. She had never been involved in any high-level sessions and was more curious than anything.

"They're pretty formal, almost like a play where all the actors already know their parts." Lynn was active in a local theater group, and Warren felt she'd understand that description. "Dr. Olsson is only two men away from the president. He has a brilliant mind. Consider a meeting with him a real compliment."

Lynn's thoughts turned to the practical. "What do you wear to these things?" For Warren, the same old suit was appropriate, but he knew Lynn probably had few dress clothes. Houston shops are no bargain centers for stylish clothing. However, he knew of one store where, Sally said, nearly new high-fashion dresses were sold at substantial savings. Lynn might find something there.

"We've got a little time before the next monitor. I'll take you shopping." He was surprised at how easily the words were spoken. She smiled and got up. "That sounds nice."

Marshall's Fashions had literally everything, so you had to know what you were looking for. As Warren knew many of the brand names, he cautioned Lynn on her choices. She disappeared into the dressing room with several outfits. Soon Lynn emerged, but for a second Warren did not recognize her. Clothes certainly do make a woman.

"Yeah, I like it. Forget those lab clothes." She had picked a suit with a carefully tailored, fitted blazer; he noticed how well her figure filled it.

"There's another one," Lynn repled. "I'll just be a minute."

Warren decided he'd certainly better classify this trip too as far as Sally was concerned. The second outfit was a loose blouson dress—slinky material, but nearly feminine.

"Well?" Lynn looked at him smiling.

"I don't know. Gosh, you look damn good in both of them." All she needed, Warren thought, was a different hair style. "We'd better get back." He was afraid one of Sally's friends might show and recognize him; that would be the frosting on the cake. He moved nervously to the front of the store to wait.

"I bought both of them," Lynn was obviously pleased. "I won't have much to eat this next week, but I'll be well dressed!" Their mood was almost festive as they returned to the base, but the monitor brought them back to reality.

"It's going down fast. I can't believe the change." Warren added the plots to his graph and extended the line one month. "If this keeps up, earth will be four degrees Fahrenheit cooler. That's enough of a change to notice at any weather station."

"Won't be much of a need to classify the project then," replied Lynn. One more day, thought Warren, and somebody sure as hell better make a decision. He was beginning to feel personally responsible for a potential global disaster.

Charlie's voice interrupted his thoughts: "We will leave tomorrow afternoon from my office at three P.M., Warren. Why don't you get some slides of that graph? That should shake 'em."

"Yessir." Warren started to elaborate, but Charlie was gone.

"I'll do it, War; I've got some other darkroom work already."

"Thanks, Lynn." Warren was grateful for the assistance.

He gave Lynn a ride home, more for moral support than anything. They were quiet for most of the trip. Warren was feeling guilty about Sally. He also knew that it would be all too easy to stop at Lynn's. But their departure was formal.

"Good night, Lynn."

"Good night, War. Thanks." The weather, he thought on his way home, was getting quite cool.

"My spaceman returns!" Sally's greeting told Warren she'd been drinking. He braced himself and walked out on the patio, where Sally, despite the cool evening, was reclining on a lounge chair.

"Hi, hon," Warren sat down and stared into the pool. God, he was tired; the strain was taking its toll. "Charlie put me on security this morning. I'm going to be away tomorrow and Friday for a meeting. That's all."

"That's all?" Sally's voice sharpened. "You're gone two whole days and all you can say is that's all? Well, I'm not sitting around this dump alone, I'll tell you." She took a long drink and got up. Her stance was unsteady, Warren noticed.

"I presume I'll see you before you leave tomorrow?"

"Yeah, hon. I'll come home to pack." He started to say, "I'll be right in," but Sally had vanished into the darkness of the house. The slam of their bedroom door echoed onto the patio, signalling another night on the couch for him. Warren got up, deciding that if food were in the offing he would have to fix something for himself. A beer and ham and cheese sandwich helped. Warren lay down on the living room couch. Now he had two uncertainties to deal with—Solar III, and his marriage.

Warren was only vaguely aware of Sally's going to work, as he got up after she left. He could and would have slept the morning. But instead he dived in the pool, swam a few lengths, and soon felt revived, even hungry. He fried some bacon and two eggs, made toast, and ate with relish. Pretty good, he thought, in spite of having to eat alone. Packing could wait; he would come home at noon for that.

Lynn was waiting for Warren at his office. "You look terrible," she commented.

"I've had nicer evenings." He was a little abrupt with her because he didn't wish to discuss the matter.

"I finished the slides; like to see them?"

"Okay, yeah." He wasn't yet able to communicate very well.

The slides were excellent and graphically showed the solar dimming theory. Lynn had extended the temperature curve one year. If the present rate continued, Houston would have an average "summer" temperature of eighteen degrees Fahrenheit. Warren hoped the reality would make an impression at the D.C. meeting. He'd also prepared a summary of the events leading up to his conclusion that solar energy was indeed decreasing and that a malfunction could not be involved.

Warren left slightly before noon to pack. His thoughts were not on home. Instead his mind was going over notes for the meeting. In a sense Warren's professional judgment was on the line. If they believed his theory, he would be famous; if not—a fool. He turned into the driveway and saw Sally was home; her car was in the garage.

"I'm home, hon." Warren decided to try a cheerful approach. "How was work this morning?"

He found her in the kitchen preparing lunch.

"I've fixed a sandwich over on the counter. Your clothes are in the bedroom."

A maid could have said it with more emotion. Well, at least a truce had been established. *I'd better leave it at that,* he thought as he headed to the bedroom. Warren placed a spare suit and change of underwear in the small valise; he had a toilet kit at the base. There was room for his papers and Lynn's slides.

"Are you going to eat?" Sally's voice came through the door. "I'm leaving."

He started out to see her, but the sound of her car leaving the garage made him stop in the kitchen. He turned to the sandwich and poured a glass of iced tea. Warren felt like something stronger, but the coming afternoon's events called for sobriety. He washed down the sandwich, grabbed the valise, and left, leaving the garage door open. The old truck coughed into life, and Warren headed for the base.

A note on his desk from Charlie's secretary gave the departure time: two thirty via car from base operations. The trip was first class. Warren hoped his presentation would be equal to the preparations. He called Lynn to check on the slides.

"I'll be right up, Warren. They're all done."

"Well, how do I look?" Lynn was standing framed in the doorway to his office. She wore one of the new dresses they'd found yesterday, and for the first time he could remember she had her hair combed in a simple pageboy.

"Wow, who are you trying to impress? You look really fantastic."

Lynn smiled. "Guess," was her reply, though the way she walked into his office answered the question. Well, if his presentation failed to make an impression, Lynn would, just by being present.

"Time to go, War." Lynn brought him back to reality.

"Yeah, well, I'll put the slides in the valise, and I'm all ready." He locked the office on the way out.

Charlie met them at operations. "Good. The limo's out here." He motioned toward a large black Cadillac waiting in front of operations. For the first time the impact of the mission registered fully with Warren; this was no ordinary critique.

"Yessir."

He picked up his valise and Lynn's bag, and the driver dropped them into a huge trunk. Lynn and Warren got into the rear seat; Charlie sat up front with the driver.

"Hanger Fourteen," Charlie ordered, and the driver nodded. They were off.

Hanger Fourteen held an impressive aircraft, a V.I.P. version of a small civilian business jet. The cabin held ten in luxury and twin engine pods bespoke its speed. Charlie disappeared into a small office and emerged with two uniformed pilots.

"Next stop D.C.—load up."

One of the pilots placed the baggage forward and opened the passenger entrance.

"The flight time will be two hours and fifteen minutes. Please fasten your seat belts during the entire trip. Food and beverages are stowed in the front firewall. Thank you."

"He sure has that memorized," Warren commented as he lowered himself into the large seat. Fastening his seat belt he leaned back and closed his eyes.

"We will be landing shortly. Please raise your seats to their upright position, extinguish smoking materials, and check that your seat belts are fastened."

Warren awoke, realizing he had slept away the entire trip.

"You missed one hell of a card game," Charlie laughed.

"Also free booze," Lynn added. Warren resented their letting him sleep, but he sure needed the rest.

"Smooth flight," was all he could reply.

They were met by an aide sent by Dr. Olsson. He was formal, routine, and brief. He reeled off his message, "Ladies will be housed in Franklin Building Forty, men in Forty-two. Here are your keys. I will pick you up at oh-eight-hundred hours tomorrow. Meals will be served at eighteen-hundred hours and oh-seven-hundred hours in the officers club, Building Thirty-Two."

Gus Olsson runs a tight ship, Charlie thought as they were whisked through the D.C. traffic with military precision. He wondered what Gus had in store for them tomorrow. Charlie had been to several of Dr. Olsson's critiques, and no two were alike. Gus knew his audience, and he usually got what he was after, often without your knowing it. Charlie decided that the trio should meet this evening to plan the presentation; being unprepared before Gus Olsson was something to be avoided.

4.
Presentation

The aide pulled up beside a quadrangle of white, two-story, angular buildings devoid of any unique architectural design save for tacked on porticoes. Nothing could disguise their origin—World War II barracks. *Ah, home,* thought Warren; he looked forward to the distinct possibility of sleeping on a bed tonight.

"I'll have your luggage delivered. You may register at reception." The aide was formal also, and his voice had an aura of authority. It made Warren nervous. "Dr. Olsson would like to see you in the officers' lounge at fifteen hundred hours." The aide and limo then vanished into the D.C. haze.

Dr. Gustav Olsson, dressed in a spotless, perfectly fitting beige suit, commanded respect automatically. He shook hands all around, but his greeting was almost abrupt.

"Welcome to Franklin Barracks. Our meeting tomorrow will include others at my invitation, and its purpose is singular. I would hope that we can resolve the problems brought to my attention by Mr. Richardson, and plan a course of action. You are, of course, to remain in this area. Any communications will be handled through my office. Your stay, I hope, will be enjoyable." Dr. Olsson made his departure. The room was silent.

Lynn was the first to speak: "Well, he's certainly in command of the situation. He'd make a great stage manager or producer. It sounds like he really knows what he's about."

"Dr. Olsson has a great deal of authority, and responsibility," commented Charlie. "Consider it a compliment to meet him."

Compliment, or not, Warren was hungry, and tired.

"Let's find out where we eat around this place."

Charlie decided to use dinner to critique their plans. "Dr. Olsson has invited others and we don't know who, or why. Warren, I'll make a few introductory remarks, then you cover the project in fifteen to twenty minutes, no longer. Lynn, you handle the slides, and make damn certain Dr. Olsson gets the full meaning of those projections. I will recap why we do not think Solar III has a malfunction, and close. If there are any questions, you take them, Warren."

Warren and Lynn nodded approval.

"Good night; see you tomorrow," Charlie called.

"Good night."

Warren and Lynn walked across the courtyard and stopped at her building.

"I feel like I'm saying good night to a college date," Warren commented. It was strange, being here with Lynn, alone. Something within him was aroused. He looked into her face for what seemed hours. Suddenly she reached up, held his head firmly with her hands, and kissed him, full, on the mouth. Almost before he could react, she turned, and was gone.

Dr. Olsson's office and staff occupied an entire floor of the energy center building, Washington D.C. at its bureaucratic best. Without substantial staff, one could not command respect.

They were ushered into one of the largest single offices Warren had ever seen. The room was dominated by a large oval table with the energy center's seal inlaid on the surface. There seemed to be a hundred chairs around it. One side of the room especially caught Lynn's attention, for it was outfitted as a small stage with lighting, public address equipment, video and slide display panels. She could visualize a press conference: "The earth, gentlemen, is freezing…" She also became aware of another person's presence in the room.

Sitting at the far end of the table was a man of indeterminable age. Fully bearded, and dressed in a heavy wool shirt, khaki trousers, and hiking shoes, he gave no indication that he was aware of them.

Dr. Olsson entered behind them.

"Good morning, please be seated." He took a chair near the stranger. "I'd like to introduce Mr. Ken Wilson."

Charlie then introduced himself, Lynn, and Warren. Ken spoke for the first time.

"Please excuse my clothing; I had no time to change. It's a long haul from the Antarctic." Charlie remembered Warren's comments that the first cooling evidence on earth would be in the polar regions.

"Mr. Wilson has been doing some center-funded work in the Antarctic. His background is in physics. I think you will find some of his recent data interesting." Dr. Olsson then motioned to the stranger.

Evidently not used to such high-level discussions, Ken Wilson was nervous. He made a crude sketch of his apparatus, showing how the expansion of the ice triggered the switch, transmitting a signal to the base. He then produced a map of his experimental area showing the positions of the instruments.

"Until ten days ago, my work was exactly as I had predicted. Note on this chart the normal daytime warming, and night cooling effects. Now look at the change here. See, all the instruments are now permanently frozen: no thawing occurs during the day.

"This next chart shows the amount of ethylene glycol I have added to prevent freezing. My increasing the amounts by as much as fifty percent did not help during the last several days.

"This last graph," he continued, "indicates my temperature changes; notice that there were no daytime fluctuations; the temperature continues to cool. I have, as I have reported to Dr. Olsson, no explanation for any of this."

The trio from Houston was dumfounded; for a moment they could not comment. Finally, Warren asked, "When did you first notice this?"

Ken checked his notes, "Twelve days ago."

That would predate the launching of Solar III; there would be no way to correlate the beginnings, Warren thought.

Dr. Olsson turned to Charlie. "Why don't you present your side of this thing now?"

Charlie introduced the Solar III project to Ken with a brief historical summary. He wanted Ken to be aware of the academic side, that the major emphasis was to gather data on the sun's energy output.

Charlie turned to Warren, "Why don't you take it from here?"

"Okay, Lynn, can you shoot some slides?" Lynn focused the first picture, a shot of Solar III just prior to liftoff. *It'd made a nice postcard,* Warren thought. The next series of slides gave the first few days of Solar III information showing the energy decrease. Warren watched Ken. He was sitting on the edge of his seat, scribbling notes on a small pad of paper.

The last slides gave the projections based on the same rate of energy loss. Summer temperatures for a number of cities had been estimated for next year. They ranged from a high of twenty degrees Fahrenheit for Miami to a low of minus thirty for New York. Warren completed his presentation by stating that the center had no answer for the solar phenomena, nor could he hazard any guess on the duration. It could end in ten days, or ten years.

"Perhaps," said Warren, "we have the dawn of a new ice age." This final remark completed their presentation.

There was silence in the room until Dr. Olsson called, "Lights, please." He moved slowly to the small podium, paused, and spoke quietly. "I have brought all of you here because it is in the national interest if we have the problem demonstrated by your separate projects. Drastic measures will have to be taken to minimize national consequences. I must also warn you that if you have erred and any of this information is released, this office will be the mockery of the executive and legislative branches of this government." Dr. Olsson paused, then continued. "It is my correct assumption, is it not, that we agree on the solar phenomena premise and rule out malfunctions or errors on your part?"

Warren recalled later that "he had our attention to such a degree we all nodded affirmative with our eyes."

From the ceiling above him, Dr. Olsson pulled a chart containing a departmental plan. "My position is here," he pointed to a block labeled "director."

"I report directly to Weld Smith, Secretary of National Energy Policy Resources. As you know, his is a cabinet post, and there is only one other level of authority. I plan to see Weld this afternoon, and what I say to him will be relayed directly to the President. Do you understand?" Once again the eyes nodded.

"I have one piece of unfortunate information for all of you; until I have received my instructions from Weld Smith, you will all remain at Franklin Base quarters." He returned to the head of the enormous table, almost lost to sight in the dimly lit room.

"Thank you," Dr. Olsson said with a sigh; the pressure was already showing.

An aide appeared from nowhere. Politely but firmly he announced, "Your transportation is ready."

Lynn's reaction was immediate; they were under guard. Her stomach felt as if she were about to go on stage on opening night. She grabbed Warren's arm.

"What are they going to do to us?"

"I don't know. Christ, I wish we'd never started this."

He found little satisfaction in Dr. Olsson's apparent acceptance of his theory; Warren almost felt he was being blamed for the whole thing.

The confinement was at least hospitable; upon their return to their quarters they were greeted with cocktails and an elegant buffet. The affair had an appearance of a travel ad, unreal.

"Hope it's not our last supper," joked Warren, followed by hollow laughter from the others.

A round of drinks helped. Ken's sense of humor increased with consumption.

"I'm lucky. I've had basic training for this. Who knows, McMurdo might turn into the Miami of the south. What do you think's going on?"

Ken looked at Charlie, who was directing his attention to a huge bowl of shrimp. He turned. "I suspect some sort of solar explosion has produced a gas, giving a dimming effect, sort of like a dust storm on earth. I've no idea how severe it is or how long this effect will last. At the rate we've measured the cooling, people will begin to notice the results damn soon."

Ken interrupted, "What's going to happen to us?"

"I dunno," Charlie mumbled between shrimp. "I suspect that matter is being worked over right now."

5.
Coverup

Weld Smith was a product of the political system. He had been governor of Texas for eight years prior to his appointment as secretary. Oil was and would always be his field of interest. Weld knew the oil interests had secured his position, and to maintain that position Weld knew what was expected of him: take care of big oil; just make certain no one got hurt.

Dr. Olsson's call interrupted Weld's usually quiet afternoon. He was hoping for a golf game. Olsson didn't play so he'd have to get rid of the doctor.

"Yes, yes, Doc, if it's short, okay, come on over."

Weld saw his golf game vanishing. "Damn eggheads, why can't they come up with this crap on Monday?"

Weld liked to end his working week on Thursday; Friday was supposed to be a day of rest before having to face his wife's weekend social spin. The coming President's deputy ball Saturday night would be miserable. They always were.

Weld's panel light showed he had a visitor. At least Doc wasted little time in getting over. "Yes, send him in."

Weld's secretary opened the heavy oak door to his office and answered, "Dr. Gustav Olsson." The door closed.

"Sit down, Doc," Weld pointed to a large cowhide-covered lounge. "You boys found something new, eh?"

"We're not certain, Mr. Smith, but some recent experiments indicate a steady loss of solar energy received on earth."

"Hey, that's good. We'll need more oil," Weld was half in jest.

"Mr. Smith," Dr. Olsson continued as if he hadn't heard Weld's interruption, "the problem is serious enough to possibly bring freezing weather to D.C. next summer. We have every reason to expect an international disaster."

"Are you serious?" Weld was waiting for the punch line.

"I have four people housed in Franklin security who presented this evidence to me today." Dr. Olsson gave Weld a brief review of the data presented by Warren and Ken. Weld stopped smiling.

"What if it's some prank—it's got to be something like that, ain't no way the sun's gonna go out like some light bulb."

"I assure you, Mr. Smith, I consider this information accurate, and of the most serious nature." Dr. Olsson's hands were shaking.

Weld looked at his golf clubs in the far corner of the office. "Wall, I'll tell ya, I reckon we ain't gonna know one way or t'uther today; I 'spect I'll just put you all under security till I think of somethin'. Don't want to take chances with them Arabs—they might be the ones tha's doin' it."

Gus couldn't tell if Weld was serious or not, often a problem when dealing with Weld Smith. Weld punched a button on his desk set.

"Class nine for Olsson and that bunch up at Franklin. I'll tell ya when to lift it." Weld turned to Dr. Gustav Olsson.

"Well, Doc, the lid's on. I got to have some time to think this one over. You'll be stayin around home now, ya hear, and keep warm!"

Class nine. Gus knew what that was. He stumbled from Weld Smith's office, and the closing of the door sounded more like steel, than wood. Twenty-four hour guard—home, lab, office, that's what class nine meant. And he didn't even know if Weld Smith believed him!

It was a somber group that assembled at Franklin that evening to hear the security briefing. Twenty-four-hour guard—they all might as well be in jail, Lynn thought.

"Can we go home?" Warren asked the security officer.

"Yes sir. You will proceed with the program, but under surveillance. You will not be allowed any movement or communication without permission. The object of this mission is to control information, and any attempt to abort security will be treated as treason. Your contact officer will be Major Jackson, this office. Any other questions?" He did not wait for an answer.

"I'm sorry." Charlie did not know what else to say. "I never knew he'd put the lid on. Christ we're the only people who know about this, and we can't do a damn thing about it."

Lynn sat down next to Warren. "I guess we'd better make the best of it, War."

He was upset to the point of being mad. "Those people out there, they should be getting ready for it. Man, they're going to freeze or starve if something isn't done. People should know!"

Ken was quiet; he was making a valiant attempt to get drunk. Being the youngest member, and a civilian in the group, Ken was not prepared at all for the events of the day. Best leave him alone, Lynn thought. She too was beginning to feel bitter; they were prisoners for telling the truth. She reached for Warren's hand, and held on tight.

The flight back to Houston was quiet, except for a card game between Warren and Charlie. Ken had been whisked away prior to their departure. It was evening now, a pale moon reflected from the wing as the last rays of the sun were left behind. As they left D.C., one additional member had joined the trio: a security guard. He sat quietly near the rear exit.

I wonder what the hell happens next, thought Lynn. She wondered about the return to Houston—would the security continue? They were all soon to have the answer to that question.

A long limousine met the late arrivals at Houston. It was dark, and a heavy overcast hung over the city, hiding the moon. *Cool for this time of the year,* thought Charlie, *damn cool.* The driver politely closed the doors, Warren heard the automatic locks click, and they were off, the security guard up front with the driver. The scene reminded him of a late TV war movie—the type where all the characters ride in black limousines and everyone salutes everyone else. This was real, however badly Warren wished it were not. It was definite reality.

Operations center, Houston, loomed ahead lit up as usual like a Christmas tree. A light rain was falling, making everything appear greasy. They were escorted from the limousine to Charlie's office. Warren noticed an additional desk and telephone had been installed.

"These boys work fast," he whispered to Lynn. She nodded, noting the changes herself. The security guard marched over to the new desk.

"Please be seated. I am Major Jackson and will be in charge of security. You and your families will be under twenty-four-hour surveillance; you are not to leave housing or travel anywhere without escort. Transportation will be provided for all your needs by this office. The code for this operation is 'ice.' Any questions will be handled by myself, or this office. That is all."

"Ice," commented Warren. "How original." He was exhausted. He looked the major in the eye.

"Uh, Major, how the hell do we get home?" Major Jackson pointed to a waiting driver, who had quietly appeared in the doorway.

"You will be escorted."

The last thing Warren remembered was the sound of those infernal limousine door locks.

"Will you please explain what's going on around here? This creep says he's going to spend the day with me." It was Sally. Warren woke up with a start. He was home.

"Hi, honey, we're being watched—came out of the D.C. trip. I didn't know any of this would happen, honest, hon."

"Well, you'd better have a better story tonight. I'm going to be late to work—hey, what's-your-name, I hope you know how the hell to drive."

Sally turned her attractive rear to Warren and grabbed the arm of a young M.P. They marched in step to a waiting limousine. He returned to Warren after seeing Sally off.

"Your limousine will be ready in forty-five minutes. Please call this number when you desire transportation from the base." He handed Warren a card with a phone number.

"Thanks." Warren left the car and aide. He still couldn't believe all that was going on around him.

The old truck stayed in the garage the next day. Warren could not remember when he'd last left it at home. Instead, the shiny, black limousine was waiting, and with a click of the door locks they were off to the base.

Changes had been made at operations, Warren noticed; a hastily built room surrounded the Solar III monitor. The door was closed. Red letters warned, "No Admittance, Security Area. Unauthorized Personnel Keep Out."

He walked down the corridor to Charlie's office, where the security officer let him pass.

"Good morning, Warren," Charlie said from across the office. "Lynn is on her way here. I'll brief you on as much as I know."

Warren was glad to see Lynn soon appear at the door.

"Hi, Lynn, how do you feel?"

"All right, I guess." She looked depressed. "I have a roommate now, nothing like making a jail out of your apartment." She sounded resigned to her fate.

Charlie spoke again: "We're all in the same boat, I've been told. Security will remain until Secretary Smith gives further instructions. We'll try to maintain business as usual around here, except that we're isolated from contact with others. Warren, daily reports from Solar III are to be code-transmitted to Dr. Olsson. Oh yes, we will eat lunch on base; they don't want to chase us around town, I suspect. Thanks for your cooperation; I really appreciate it."

"You're welcome," Warren said as he and Lynn left for the monitor.

The security guard checked their I.D. cards and opened the monitor room door. Upholstered chairs and a work table complete with a shiny new coffee pot made up the interior, along with the monitor. There was no telephone.

"Well, let's see what's happened to ol' sol." Warren punched the display block. Rows of numbers appeared, white against a green background.

"Wow, they're dropping fast," Lynn commented. "They won't need to keep this a secret for long; people are going to feel the effect soon."

"They won't know the cause, though, and they'll think it's only freak weather," answered Warren. "They have a right to know the truth—they should be told."

Warren felt yesterday's bitterness returning. He'd never completely accept the concept of security. The whole idea he associated with war, and conflict.

"I'll plot this and get it coded for D.C.," Lynn said as she started the process procedure. "Pour me a cup of coffee, War." He passed a hot cup of coffee to her, then made a brief system check. As usual, Solar III was performing flawlessly, as far as they could determine.

A separate table had been set in the cafeteria for lunch. Warren, Lynn, Charlie, and Major Jackson ate in silence for the most part. The presence of the security officer limited conversation to niceties.

"How's the monitor, Warren?"

"Okay, Charlie, still going down. Lynn is coding and transmitting to D.C."

Charlie handed a memo to Warren. "I've cut off the university program. Had to. Couldn't risk their knowing anything."

Warren read the contents. Charlie had explained that a faulty positioning rocket had fired, sending the satellite suborbital. It had burned to a cinder. As much as he disliked the university team and Professor Fellstrom, this was an outright lie. Charlie noticed his resentment.

"It had to be done. I had no choice in the matter." A glance from Major Jackson warned Charlie to end the discussion.

"Cool weather we're having," was the best Charlie could do for a closing.

Warren had noticed that the only time he and Lynn were left alone was in the monitor room. He hoped they hadn't bugged it.

"Lynn, I've got to get out somehow. People out there have got to be told the truth."

She looked at him kindly. "War, I know, but they'd think you were crazy. You would be locked up before you could convince anyone. Think of your career and Sally; you could never work in this field again."

"Lynn, if this thing is for real, none of us will have to worry about work. We won't be alive. Think of the food problem. Without the sun's heat, there will be no food anywhere next year. If people knew, they could at least cut down consumption, or store supplies. We don't know how long this thing is going to last—they might make it."

Lynn gave him a strange glance. She had never thought of Warren as a crusader, yet the events of the last few days could alter anybody's attitude. They had always had almost unlimited freedom and the thought of losing it never entered their minds. However, there was some logic to the secrecy, she felt. After all, if the whole matter was the result of a malfunction, why start a world panic? Was Warren's and her concern over world implications, or simply over loss of their personal freedom? She couldn't answer that one truthfully at this time.

"I don't know how I feel, War. I've got to think it over." She poured herself a cup of coffee and stared blankly at the monitor. The afternoon waned on.

The limousine lumbered to a halt in Warren's drive; he wondered what the neighbors thought of all the traffic. Sally's figure was silhouetted in the kitchen window, the evening sunset behind her. Too cool for a swim. Dammit, it *was* cool, not just a figment of his imagination.

"Good night, sir." The driver was waiting for him to exit.

"Thanks." Warren walked up the drive.

Sally was preparing supper. He noticed an extra place set at the table.

"Hi, hon, have a nice day?"

"If being followed all over town is your idea of a nice time, yes. When do I get clued in on the rules of the game?"

"I'm sorry, hon, I just haven't had time. I don't know much more than you."

Warren gave Sally a rundown of the events leading up to the security clampdown. He noticed that the guard was listening.

"Let's go to the bedroom," Warren whispered. "That guy's listening."

They closed the door, and he turned on the shower. If the room were bugged that would cover the sound of their voices.

"Look, hon, we've got to get the hell out of here. The world's going to freeze up fast if this sun thing keeps on. If we can get a stash of food before the rest of..."

Sally interrupted him. "You're out of your mind!" She wasn't whispering. "This whole thing is crazy, and you know it. I'll tell you one thing you'd damn well better do—get me out of whatever you've done, and fast. A couple more days of that creep out there following me, and I'm out of a job, and I didn't spend the last five years pushing for a bust."

The conversation ended with her slamming the bedroom door; he was alone.

"Hell, I tried." Warren half spoke the words. The running water reminded him how good a hot shower might feel; he undressed and soaked the warmth of the spray for almost a half hour. He wrapped up in a robe for dinner.

Sally was politely quiet during the meal. She served the guard first, then Warren; the guy was a guest of sorts. Warren never knew his name. After the meal, Warren took his coffee to the den to watch the TV news and weather. Sally and the guard followed. The usual news of world unrest was first, then the weather.

"Record cool temperatures are being felt, particularly in the Northeast. Local farmers in Maine fear for the potato crop."

The announcer penciled a few examples on a large plastic outline map of the U.S. All recordings were in the low thirties. Warren glanced at Sally; if she had any concern she did not show it. He figured maybe two more weeks or so and reports such as the one he'd just seen would be commonplace. It would be difficult to hide the fact that something was amiss; too many people watched the network news.

"I'm going to turn in. Long day. G'night all." It was a little awkward not knowing the guard's name, but it'd probably be someone else tomorrow anyway.

He was asleep as soon as he lay down; Warren did not hear Sally enter and crawl in beside him. (She would never tell Warren how scared she was.) When he awoke, she was already gone. Sally taped an evening show on Sunday morning for a monthly fashion review; this must be the day, he thought.

A brief swim under a cool, overcast sky refreshed him. As he fixed breakfast, Warren wondered where the guard was. He then noticed him standing in the drive looking at the gray sky. Warren knew that if he were to make any attempt at escape he had to do it soon. Time was running out. How, he wondered, was he going to convince Sally to take the risk. Warren had no answer to that problem.

He was almost glad when Monday's limousine picked him up for the trip to the base; the weekend had raised more questions than answers. Warren was anxious to see Lynn; the monitor room had become their refuge.

She poured coffee for the two of them. "What did you do this weekend?" she asked. Warren told of his attempt to tell Sally.

"Lynn, I want to get out. Somehow I'm going to find a way. I started this mess and nobody is going to cork it in a bottle forever. Someone out there will listen—if I could only get on one TV talk show." He was thinking of the weather report last Saturday night.

"We're covered, day and night," she replied. "They'd spot you in a minute."

"Hell, I know that. I mean, look, please help me think of a way."

Lynn smiled. "Another cup of coffee?"

"Yeah, thanks. I'm sorry, guess it's getting to me." The last person he wanted to argue with was Lynn.

She nodded. "Let's get caught up with the data; you monitor, I'll code."

Charlie met them for lunch and gave each of them a copy of a memo from Weld Smith to Dr. Gustav Olsson. "Ice" had been given national security priority: all parties involved were being transferred to D.C. The military and security were taking over.

"I can't say what they will do with us up there; I suspect some sort of confinement."

Charlie looked to Major Jackson for comment, but there was none. Warren had known something like this was coming. It would be too difficult keeping long-term security at the base. Sooner or later other personnel would find out what was going on. If he was going to make a move, he'd best be on with it. Time was getting short.

"I have an idea." Lynn pulled her chair beside his at the monitor. "War, you need a disguise. I have my theater makeup kit at home. If I could get it here we could change your face. They wouldn't know."

"No, Lynn, there're too many security checks here; we'd have to change base I.D. cards, everything. Thanks Lynn, but there's not enough time."

The idea, though, stuck with him on his way home.

Sally was cordial, better than she had been in several days. She seemed to understand something of what he was going through. He offered to grill steaks.

"Fix me a drink, hon," Warren called from the patio. The new guard was with him.

"Nice pool. Wish the weather was warmer. I'd take a swim."

"Yeah, it is nice." Warren turned the steaks and the grill flared briefly. Sally handed him a drink, and as he sipped it, the Scotch revived him. Maybe, as Sally had said, he was crazy to think of leaving all of this for an unknown crusade which could turn into a mission of folly.

"Steaks are done, hon." Warren covered the grill, bringing a plate of sizzling meat to the table. One advantage of Texas, he thought, good meat. They always assumed that steaks were as close as the shopping center. *Would it be that way a year from now?* he wondered. He drained his drink.

Warren decided to watch the weather and news again; he was beginning to develop a morbid fascination for the revealing data.

"Five days of record cold temperatures reported from Mt. Washington, New Hampshire. No relief in sight. Early harvests could cut farm production by fifteen per cent," the announcer reported.

He thought of calling Lynn, but decided against it because the guard might report his action. The less known the better, Warren felt.

Tonight, Sally accompanied him to bed.

"Do you have something to do with that weather report?" she asked.

"I'm not sure, hon, but I think it's a result of the cooling."

Sally gave him a long look. "This is for real? I mean no kidding now."

"I don't know." Warren sat down on the bed. "That's the hell of it. We don't know."

The food and drink made him groggy; his mind did not respond to the challenge.

"Think I'll shower, Sal. I'm tired."

He started toward the bath, but she was not finished. "What will happen to us?"

He turned on the shower before his answer: "Our only chance is to somehow get out of here—leave everything, and try to reach another country. I've no plan yet. I don't even know where we'd go."

He could tell by her expression she did not care for the idea.

"I know one thing," she spoke slowly. "I am not leaving this house. I've done nothing illegal—nothing. I'm up to here with these goons. Why don't you tell Charlie, or whoever is responsible for this, that you're through unless they cut this crap out."

"God, hon, I wish it were that simple. I'm involved all the way to the top. They'll put me away before they take any rap. You know how it is with the government." The steam from the shower was overwhelming. Warren stepped into the cauldron and closed the glass door.

"One of the things you learn in this game, I reckon, is to make the best of others' troubles; hell, that's half of being a politician!" Weld Smith's thoughts sent him to a small card file hidden in his credenza. "Wallace C. Redding, Chairman, Petroleum International Properties, Inc., Dallas, Texas." He dialed the number on his private phone. "Weld Smith for W.C."

The secretary's voice sounded as if she were in a large room. "One moment, Mr. Secretary, for Mr. Redding."

"Hello, hi Weld, you old SOB; how's thing up there in D.C.?" Wallace's voice commanded, and received, attention.

"Damn good W.C. Say, something came across the desk the other day—thought you might like to know about it—reckon it could be useful."

"Fine, Weld. That's why we have you up there—to be real useful to us poor folks back home." Laughter followed W.C.'s comment.

"Well, here's the deal." Weld enjoyed the scoop. "One of my eggheads came up with a story the sun's sinkin' or somethin'. Anyway, it's gonna be real cold this winter, and some folks gonna be needing a lot of fuel to stay warm; y'all understand?"

"Keep goin'," W.C. boomed.

"Well, I got it figured if you start holdin' back on oil now you can be pretty damn sure of a good price increase for a Christmas present. We could jus' possibly cook up a little ol' energy crises for you."

"For real?—You're sure it's for real?" W.C. didn't like working for nothing—he lost money that way, and W.C. hated losing money.

"Tip's good, W.C. I got a lid on it so there won't be no leaks. It's all yours."

"Well, I shore do thank y'all—ya know that little place in Nassau you been lookin' to buy? Well, you just plan on it being *your* Christmas present. How 'bout that?"

Weld was overjoyed, a dream home, and all it took was one phone call.

"Sure nice to do business with you, W.C. Sure do appreciate it." W.C. clicked off, and Weld leaned back in his huge leather chair and smiled. The good life.

6.
Escape

A note and check greeted Warren, placed beside the coffee pot by Sally. "Please pay Emilo before he leaves, thanks, S." Emilo was their Mexican gardener; he would arrive at sunrise and work in the cool of the early morning. His wife picked him up around eight o'clock. Warren envied him—no cares, enough money to live on, and the day free. Who said Mexicans were dumb?

The security guard, cup of coffee in hand, was staring out on the patio, watching Emilo cleaning the pool.

"Want some more coffee?" Warren offered the pot.

"Yeah, thanks." The guy sounded half asleep.

Wonder if I could overpower him, Warren thought. *Then what? Hell, I wouldn't get two blocks away from here.* The thought chilled him; he was beginning to realize his desperation. On his way out to the waiting limousine he handed Emilo his check. The Mexican nodded; he spoke no English at all.

The limousine halted. Ahead two Mexicans were locked in argument over a collision.

"Hell, the cars are so battered how can they tell where the damage is?" Warren muttered. The limousine driver did not answer. *Another silent type,* cursed Warren. *Mexicans, damn Mexicans, they're taking us over.*

The thought hit him hard. That was *it*—Mexicans! If he could pass as a Mexican, they'd never find him. Emilo—hell, he could be Emilo, and walk away from those bastards. But Sally, how was he going to convince her? Warren saw the gate pass by; the guard waved. He'd have to come back for her somehow. Maybe after everyone knew, they would have no reason for all this security. It was a risk he'd have to take. The click of the door locks brought him back to the reality of the base. They had arrived.

Warren went to the monitor room. He hoped Lynn would be there, but instead Charlie was watching the screen.

"Incredible! No wonder we've had cool weather! Look at that damn thing drop!"

"I know," Warren added. "But why all this security? The news media already has caught on to the fact that something strange is happening. It's only a matter of time."

"Don't question it, Warren. The fact remains we are under orders. We have our job, they have theirs."

Warren nodded and sat down. Where was Lynn? He had to talk to her about his plan. He poured a cup of coffee and stared into the murky depths of the hot fluid.

"Hi, everybody." It was Lynn. "How goes the program?"

"Take a look." Warren moved away from the monitor. "Pretty bad, huh?"

"Gosh, it sure is going down fast. Wait till D.C. gets this update!" Lynn seemed almost pleased as she started to process. Finally, a light on the page board glowed—central wanted Charlie. They were alone.

Warren watched the door for a moment; then he turned to Lynn and said, almost in a whisper, "I've got a plan."

He outlined his idea of replacing Emilo, the gardener. He could disguise himself as the Mexican. He could then leave on his own with a chance of getting across the border before the security guard knew of his absence. If Lynn could show him how to apply the makeup, he could do the transformation at home during the night. He'd leave a note telling Sally he had been called to the base. If she didn't talk to the guard it might just work. A lot of ifs, but it was the best scheme Warren could come up with, and time was running out.

He watched for Lynn's reaction. "Do you think I've got a chance?"

She didn't answer for a moment, then: "Do you really want to do it? It's an awful chance."

"Yes, dammit, for once I'm going to do something on my own, without asking permission from anyone. The whole place can go straight to hell; I want out."

Lynn avoided his anger for a moment. Then she faced Warren and asked, "What about me?"

She shot from the hip; Warren had not included her in his plans. The omission was not selfish, he just had not considered involving her.

"I'll help you," she continued, "on one condition. I go with you." Her face was set, stern; he had no choice.

"Yeah, how I don't know, but if you want to leave, I won't stop you."

Warren knew he couldn't stop Lynn. He'd confided in her, and confidence made them partners. They were joined together by that continuing flow of data from Solar III; earth *was* cooling, the theory of solar dimming was reality.

"When do you want to go?"

They were back in the monitor room after lunch when Lynn asked the question.

"Emilo's day off is Thursday," Warren answered. "That's the only day we've got. I'll have to chance that the guard doesn't know his schedule."

"His wife picks him up before you leave," Lynn smiled. "I'll be your wife; my old car will pass for anything a Mexican gardener might own."

She checked the door; it was locked.

"The makeup kit will fit in your attache case. They don't check that, do they?"

"No, so far they haven't," he replied.

"All I can do here is explain the process," she cautioned. "You'll have to do it right the first time."

Lynn spent most of the afternoon going over makeup details with Warren. They were interrupted once when Charlie wanted a recode, and Warren was a little nervous after the visit.

"I'll go back to my office now. I don't want Charlie getting any ideas."

She locked the door after him. Events were moving a little faster than expected; one more day, and there was no turning back.

Warren packed the makeup kit in his attache case while Lynn checked the hall. The long row of lockers reminded him of his high school—deserted except between classes when the halls were mobbed.

"Okay, I'm through." he closed the locker door, and the two of them slowly walked the long length of the hall. Their journey had begun.

The limousine ride home seemed endless; nobody had questioned Warren about the attache case, yet the thought of its contents made him nervous. He was relieved when his driveway appeared—home. Sally was on the patio, drink in hand. It was not her first.

"This guard type doesn't drink—he's A.A. or somethin'."

"Hi, hon." He looked around the patio; the guard was nowhere in sight.

"Think I'll take a swim."

Warren felt the silence for a moment, then exited to the bedroom to suit up. He left the attache case in the hall.

"God, the water's cold," Warren cursed. "Wish the sun would shine a little bit." He knew the answer to that one—it would only become colder. Warren looked over toward Sally; she was silent, staring into an empty glass.

"Come in!" He splashed her in fun. But Sally was in no mood for humor. Warren ducked as the cocktail glass sailed by his head. She got up and disappeared into the kitchen, hips swaying in defiance. He swam several lengths before retiring to a hot shower.

Lacking conversation, Warren switched on the television. A twenty-year-old Western rattled across the screen. It took his mind off the project. The news followed. Warren's interest picked up. Most of the weather stations were reporting record low readings, and a feature story gave time to a farmer in upstate New York whose crops had been destroyed by the early cold. *There will be many more just like him*, Warren thought.

"Dinner," Sally called. He looked around to see her, somewhat unsteadily, setting dishes on the table. The guard appeared for the first time, another new face. Warren got up with reluctance; he wasn't particularly hungry. One more evening at home and he was leaving, possibly forever. The attache case was visible in the hall where he had left it; he wished he'd placed it out of sight.

Lynn met him at his office the next morning. "War, they've locked the monitor. What's going on?"

"I don't know; I just got here. You seen Charlie?" He was afraid that time was running out, fast.

"No," she replied. "Let's go up and find him."

They met Charlie at the landing.

"Christ, what gives?" Warren almost shouted the words.

"We're being transferred out tomorrow—all of us—to D.C. The project is being taken over by security; we're finished." Charlie's face fell with the words. They all knew it had been coming, but the reality of it hurt. They had been guilty only of a scientific mission, well executed, and honestly reported. This was their profession; if it now became a criminal act, what was left? Charlie tried to console them.

"I know it's a rotten deal. You've done a fantastic piece of work. I want you to believe that I had no choice—they just told me what to do."

Warren nodded. "Thanks, Charlie." He couldn't think of anything else to say.

Warren and Lynn spent most of the day packing up records to be impounded. As each box was filled and labeled, security moved it to a waiting van.

"Damn efficient bastards, aren't they," Warren commented. Lynn gave him a faint smile. There was too much on her mind for much conversation. She had to make her own escape and get to Warren, all before anyone noticed their absence. She had the more difficult task, and if they failed…She put the thought out of her mind. They had to succeed. Lynn put her mind to the packing effort; being busy was better than thinking.

They left the office separately, but before Warren left to meet his limousine she pressed a piece of paper in his hand and squeezed it hard. In the privacy of the car Warren glanced at the note—"Walk south on Piedraes, watch for me."

She was smart; south would be in the opposite direction taken by the morning limousine. Beyond that, what she had planned was a mystery. Lynn had probably meant to discuss their escape in detail, but the loss of the monitor room cut their only line of communication. It was up to her to make the plan a success. The limousine groaned to a stop; he was home.

Sally was preparing dinner when Warren arrived, his favorite—Mexican tacos. It struck Warren as a curious last supper. A few hours, and the reality of leaving his life behind him would begin.

"Sure smells good, hon," Warren felt his voice crack under the strain.

She nodded. "Better set the table for me. I'm about ready."

"Okay, hon." Warren set the usual three places; although he hadn't seen the guard, he felt his presence. It was too cold to consider eating on the patio. Frost was predicted for the evening—something unheard of for that time of year in Houston.

"Damn the sun," he spoke under his breath as the dishes and silverware rattled into place. The security guard was watching him from outside the patio; Warren caught his shadow for a moment. *You'd have to be a peeping Tom to hold down that job,* he thought to himself.

The meal passed in silence for Warren; he concentrated on the tacos even though his usual keen appetite was missing. The guard was from Chicago and disliked hot Mexican food; he made a valiant attempt to eat by washing down his food with copious amounts of water. Warren hoped the guard would sleep in spite of it all. After the meal, the guard helped Warren cover the patio flowers with newspaper to prevent frost damage. It was a miserable evening; the dampness penetrated to the bone. Warren thanked him for his help, but otherwise the task was completed in silence.

Warren switched on the TV and another Western held forth; he was not interested, and instead concentrated on trying to remember Lynn's makeup instructions. He had to do it right the first time; no second chance existed.

The attache case was in the bedroom, beside the small desk. Warren would have to make up between three and four o'clock in the morning, without the alarm clock, dress, apply makeup, and somehow get outside unseen by the guard. Talk about an impossible task—this was it! He climbed into bed, and in spite of his thoughts, fell asleep.

He would never have awakened save for the barking of the neighbor's dog. It was 3:30 A.M. Perhaps the guard got the dog aroused. Sally was sound asleep; thank goodness for that. Warren selected his oldest set of yard-work clothes and carried the attache case into the bathroom. There was no outside window—he would work unnoticed.

The makeup was almost fun; Warren watched his face slowly change to that of a mustached Mexican. The black dye and oil on his hair looked perfect; his confidence was improving. Warren slipped the attache case under the towel cabinet, turned off the light, and carefully opened the door. Sally was still asleep. He grabbed his passport, wallet, and watch from his desk, then crept to the window to listen for the guard. The sky was turning faintly red in the east. He could see the guard, over by the patio, resting in a poolside chair. Feet first, Warren let himself out through the window and dropped behind the cover of the bushes. The guard did not stir. But there would be another guard in a car by the front curb. There was a hose coil and sprinkler beside the garage; he would have to become the gardener to avoid suspicion.

Warren picked up the coil and sprinkler, then slowly walked toward the front of the house. He let the hose reel uncoil and set the sprinkler on the front terrace. The guard in the car was watching him. Warren connected the hose to the water outlet, and turned the valve on. The guard appeared to lose interest. Warren glanced at his watch; it was 4:30 A.M., and cold. He started weeding the patio border; from that vantage point Warren had a good view of both guards. He had an hour and a half before Sally would awake and miss him. Warren worked his way along the border toward the street, trying to watch the movement of the guards; the man on the patio was gone.

"Nice morning eh?" Warren's heart stopped; the guard was directly behind him, speaking.

Warren's face paled beneath the makeup. He turned slowly.

"Si?"

The guard looked at him. "You speak English?"

Warren managed a "No, señor," smiled, and turned to his weeding. It had been a good try. To his immense surprise the guard was leaving. He could hear his footsteps retreating toward the car. Still shaking, Warren watched as he opened the car door and joined his partner; they were opening a jug of coffee, and more important, they were not watching him. Warren made his way slowly down the hedge border to the street. He moved quickly to the other side and started down Piedraes Street, South. Warren did not look behind him; there was no turning back.

For Lynn the escape was more complex; she had to find transportation for the two of them. Security knew her car; she would have to locate another. Lynn had managed to withdraw most of her savings through the mail, and the security guards had not suspected anything as far as she could tell. Clothing and food would have to be purchased, along with any travel necessities. Lynn planned to disguise herself as a Mexican domestic servant and purchase a used car from a lot about three blocks from her apartment. The dealer was used to cash transactions, particularly with Mexicans. She could get a car that was in running condition for a few hundred dollars, no questions asked. Lynn planned to change the plate numbers on her own car, using red grease paint, and take the license plates with her. She had parked her car at the far end of the apartment lot; she hoped the guard would not spot her removing the plates. The number AC-7343 would be altered to AO-7848; the combination of a different car and license number might give them time to reach the border. Once out of Houston they would be hard to spot.

Lynn had one advantage over Warren; the guard left her alone for the most part in her apartment and seemed content with watching the door and immediate yard. She placed the alarm clock, set for 5:00 A.M., under her pillow, and left her makeup equipment in the bathroom. Her exit would be through a small kitchen window opening onto the alley. The darkness would hide her until she was certain the guard was out of sight. But that was all for tomorrow; her mind slowed and Lynn fell asleep, easily.

Warren had maintained a moderate pace since leaving home; there were a number of Mexicans on the street, and he would have been almost impossible to spot.

Piedraes was a through street, busy with commuter traffic even at this early hour. At one time it had been a quiet residential road, but the base had changed all of that. It seemed that every day a new fast food shop or self-service gasoline station appeared on a corner lot previously occupied by a home. Warren had thought of moving, but the cost of a new home was beyond their means without selling their present house for a healthy price. Perhaps, one day, the pressure of the commercial strip would present a buyer. So preoccupied was Warren with his thoughts that he barely noticed a battered sedan pull over to the curb. At the wheel was a middle aged Mexican domestic. Her face was lined from the years of toil. Yet he distinctly heard his name called.

"War, War, over here, quick!" He stopped and stared at the car. Christ, it was Lynn. She held the door open for him. He could hardly believe it.

She laughed. "I'm glad you wore the red shirt, I'd never have recognized you."

"But where, how did you do it, get this car and all?" Warren was amazed at her pluck.

Lynn explained her plan as they continued down the thoroughfare. The car had cost her $250; the altered license plates would deter anyone from stopping them for the present. She spoke with pride of her accomplishments as they moved with the early morning traffic. It was strange not going the usual route to the base. The car lurched and rattled, yet responded to the accelerator with an agility belying its years. Warren guessed the age and model as a '52 or '53 Chevrolet.

"Hope this heap makes it to the border." He laughed as he spoke. Lynn gave him a smile.

"Best deal on the lot, all new skins. And an overhaul, at least that's what he said."

The sign loomed—Victoria and south ahead. They were on their way.

7.
Fugitive

Weld Smith lowered his frame into the luxury of the leather seat and stared at his golf bag, still in the corner. Today, come hell or high water, he was going to put those clubs to use. The phone buzzer brought his thoughts up short—damn security line.

"Hello. Yes, this is Smith—what the hell! They're both gone? Jesus Christ, what kind of idiots ya'll got down there? Well, you damn well better find them, or I got a replacement for the whole damn bunch of ya'll." He slammed the receiver hard. *Shit* was all Weld's mind could deliver; *shit*. Warren and Lynn were now among the hunted. It was 8:30 A.M. Houston time.

Weld Smith's coarse order brought an almost instant response from Houston base security. Within thirty minutes, commuters were cursing the long traffic lines caused by the roadblocks. The manhunt was on.

Warren and Lynn had missed the initial security attempts. They'd had enough of a head start so as to be outside of the Houston city limits. The car had settled into a fifty-mile-an-hour pace as they passed the sign—Victoria—ninety miles. For the first time they took stock of their possessions. Old clothes, passports, Lynn's money, the car, and makeup kits.

"We better get rid of the makeup kit. If we're stopped it's a dead giveaway." Warren started to roll down the window.

"No." Lynn stopped him. "We will have to touch ourselves up before Laredo. They'll have the border posted—we'll have to chance their letting us through."

Red flashing squad car lights ahead ended the discussion. Warren jammed the damning evidence under the front seat.

"Let me talk," Lynn cautioned. "Whatever happens, don't say a word." They slowed to a halt, and a tall, tanned state trooper surveyed them from a respectable distance, then walked toward Lynn's window. She cranked it down with some difficulty, and before the trooper could speak, started a babble of Spanish totally incomprehensible to Warren. The trooper withstood the barrage for a minute, then, with a look of resignation, waved them on.

It was some time before Warren found his voice. "Fantastic, what did you say to him?"

Lynn was obviously pleased with her performance. "I told him you were my husband, and that you were also deaf. We've been visiting friends in Houston—that's all." Warren stared at her for a moment: He was seeing, for the first time, a side of Lynn that was to become increasingly important: she was both resourceful and courageous.

They made a rest stop in Victoria at an old, battered filling station which obviously catered to Mexican workers. Two outhouses, their doors banging in the cool, dry wind, were the only accommodations.

"Take your makeup kit with you. We may not get another chance before the border." Lynn handed Warren a small mirror as she spoke.

Somehow he managed to latch the door, and after his eyes became accustomed to the dim light, he made a few repairs to his face. Warren felt dirty with all the grease paint layered over his skin, yet he knew it was their only chance to survive. They had to get across the border; once in Mexico they would be reasonably safe traveling as Americans.

"Want me to drive?" Warren offered.

"No, thanks," Lynn laughed. "You're deaf—remember?" The engine coughed back to life, and their trip continued.

"I never dreamed they'd pull something like that." Charlie was talking to Dr. Olsson. "They never told me anything."

"I believe you, Charlie. I just hope you understand my position up here. Smith has been in a rage all morning over this, and he's sure we're all involved."

"Christ, Gus, I'm sorry, but I don't know a damn thing—even Belting's wife didn't have a clue."

"Okay, okay, Charlie, just don't move off that base till I get back to you, okay?"

"Yessir, yes, I understand, yeah, goodbye, Gus." Charlie put his head in his hands. He was close to tears. An entire career shot to hell, all because of some lousy data. He didn't blame Warren and Lynn for what they'd done; he almost wished he were with them at this point.

It was dusk as the fugitives neared Laredo, an orange Texas sunset colored by the dust. A few lights shone—how they envied those who could stop for a hot shower and a soft, warm bed. Warren and Lynn could see the radio towers now—Mexico. They had to get across that border tonight. It was a strange feeling, being hunted in one's own country, not being able to move freely. They were aliens in the true sense of the term. America was behind them now. No return to any part of that which, until a few hours ago, had been taken for granted. The American way.

Lynn stopped the car several blocks from the border.

"Let's walk up to the bridge and watch for a while." Somehow she knew what she was doing, Warren thought as he followed. The route was crowded with a mixture of Mexicans returning home and American tourists gearing up for a night in old Mexico. To many, Mexico was the border town, night life, souvenir shops, cheap liquor. Nothing else probably mattered.

"Watch the customs guards, War," Lynn pointed to the inspection point. A steady line of cars was passing with what seemed a minimum of delay. A quick glance at the auto's interior, and passage was allowed. They could not see the other end of the bridge, yet no traffic delays were visible.

"We could walk across," Warren suggested. "They don't even stop those people."

"We need that car," Lynn reminded him. "We don't stand a chance without it." She was, as usual in such matters, correct.

"Christ, it's cold out here." Warren's old shirt was less than adequate for the chill. "Let's go back to the car."

Lynn was lost in thought on the walk back to their parking spot. She was working out strategy.

"War, we should split up for the crossing; they'll be looking for a couple—one person in the car would attract less attention."

"But how?" Warren countered. "Hell, as soon as I speak I'm a goner. You know I can't speak one word of Spanish."

"The trunk." Lynn watched for a moment to make certain they were not being observed. She tried the rusty lock.

"Get in! Quickly." Without thinking, he obeyed. The lid slammed him into darkness. A moment later they were under way.

"Mr. Smith," Weld's secretary called from the outer office. "Secretary Sands to see you, sir." Weld bolted upright. The Secretary of State was one man who could put the fear of God in Weld Smith.

"Yessir, Mister Secretary, come right in." Roger Sands walked, spoke, and commanded authority. He ran the country for all practical purposes, and he compensated for a weak president.

"I'll come to the point. Weld. There are several news stories concerned with this horrible cold spell we're having—they imply we're hiding something. I would assume your group would know if we know anything at all."

Weld tried not to act stunned. "What kind of stories, Mr. Secretary?"

"Most deal with some theory surrounding loss of some of the sun's heat." Roger was firm, correct in his manner. "We will have to make a statement to confirm, or deny."

Weld knew who "we" referred to—the office of the President. Damn news hounds. He had a leak somewhere, and they had found it. This would blow his oil deal; without the backing of Petroleum International, he was done. "W.C." could pull his cork any time he damn well pleased. Weld decided to lie, as usual.

"Nothin' that we know about, Mr. Secretary. Must be one of those Yankee winters we get every fifty years." Secretary Sands listened, and stared through him for a moment. Then with a polite "thank you," he made a formal exit. Weld sat down and noticed that his hands were shaking.

The combination of dust and exhaust fumes were taking their toll on Warren. He tried to hear over the clatter of the car, but it was hopeless. Twice, he could have sworn someone tried to open the trunk lid. The car would stop, move a few feet, and stop again. They were in the lineup for inspection, but had they made it? The fumes made him sick and groggy. He felt himself drifting off to sleep.

"War! Oh, thank heaven. I'm sorry, I just couldn't get through any faster." He was in a field beside a road looking into Lynn's face. She had been giving him mouth to mouth resuscitation. She stopped, then kissed him. Color returned to his face.

"What happened? Where are we?" She must have made it across, somehow.

"Can you walk?" Lynn asked. He got up, dizzy, but she helped him over to the car. It was dark, and from the view of the lights behind them they were several miles south of Nuevo Laredo, Mexico. Lynn looked at him with some concern. It had been a close call. Warren saw her concern and squeezed her hand.

"I'm okay now; just tell me what happened." She put the car in gear as she spoke. They were headed south—Monterrey, Mexico.

"After I closed you in the trunk, I got in line behind two Mexican cars." Lynn stopped to pull the headlight switch on—it worked. "I told the customs official I was employed in Houston and returning to Monterrey to visit a sick father. He wasn't expected to live, and I was in a hurry. When the guard asked me to open the trunk, I told him that the lock was rusty and it would not open. He tried to pull on the handle, but the lock held."

Warren stopped her. "I heard someone working on it; Christ, I thought I'd had it."

Lynn continued, "It seemed like hours getting over the bridge, but on the Mexican side the guard let me pass with just a wave. My makeup was starting to smear, and if he'd looked at me any closer I don't think I would have passed as Mexican."

"Fantastic!" Warren shared Lynn's feeling of victory. "Where do we go tonight, though?" Lynn smiled for the first time since their crossing.

"Monterrey," was all she said.

It was well past midnight when they pulled into a small motel on the outskirts of Monterrey. Beneath the neon sign "El-Reo," a small red word flickered "Hay Cuartos." The sound of a brass band came from a small bar, mingled with the voices of a clientele well on their way to a good drunk. There would be a number of headaches to nurse come morning.

The jangle of the desk bell resulted in the appearance of a Mexican, half asleep, but evidently the night clerk.

"Yes?" He spoke English with an eastern accent.

"We'd like a room." Lynn spoke in broken English. "For tonight."

"Si, yes, of course." The clerk turned to the board behind him and selected one of a half-dozen remaining keys.

"Number twenty-six. That will be eleven dollars, please." Warren pulled a ten and a one dollar bill from his wallet and pocketed the key, and they left the clerk to his sleep.

"I hope it's heated; it's damn cold out here," Warren said as he felt the damp night air penetrate his shirt. It was close to freezing. They drove slowly down the row of fake adobe units and pulled the car into the parking space in front of "No. 26."

Warren suddenly realized his predicament: he, a married man, was about to spend a night with another woman. True, he had one hell of a story, but nonetheless the reality shocked him. He hesitated at the door.

Lynn reached in front of him and tried the knob. It was unlocked. The room inside was plain, painted in a pale pink, with white curtains and vintage Hollywood bed and dresser set. The only new item was a color TV set, chained to a wall bracket.

"God, I can't wait to get this grease off," Lynn sighed. She opened her makeup kit and used some tissue to blot the smearing paint. "Here, work on your face, War." She handed him several tissues.

Warren was exhausted from the trip. The effects of his experience in the trunk was having its effect.

"May I wash first?" he asked.

"Sure, make yourself at home," Lynn replied with her usual smile.

Warren adjusted the rust-stained faucets in the shower stall. Clouds of steam exited from behind the curtain. The warm vapor drugged him as he piled his clothes on the toilet seat. How nice it would be to have something clean for a replacement, but that would have to wait until tomorrow. He let the hot water soak him and remove the dirt and strain of the day.

Lynn's voice came through the noise of the shower: "Hey, save some for me!"

"Okay, I'm through," Warren called back as he reluctantly shut the water off. He pulled his shorts on and draped the old shirt over his shoulders. "It's all yours."

"Thanks," Lynn replied as the door closed behind her. Soon the sound of the shower came through the wall. The thought of her in there, unclothed, excited him. Warren turned down the bed and was asleep within minutes. It was two o'clock in the morning when he awoke. The sun was low over the desert, sending red rays through the window which seemed to set the room on fire. He became gradually aware of Lynn's presence beside him. She had pulled herself close, and Warren became immediately aware that she had nothing on. For a few moments he resisted, feigning sleep, and then he could stand it no longer. Warren turned into her waiting arms. God, how he wanted her. The tensions of the past day left him and were replaced by a feeling of quiet security.

Of their actual act, Warren could remember little. Reality was yet to be totally separated from dreams.

They lay together afterwards, watching the color of the room change from red to the pale light of a cold, cloudy day. Frost sparkled on the windows. Even the room was chilled. The motel had not been designed for such cold.

"What time is it?" Lynn asked. She didn't want to know, but the practical side of her mind was at work.

"Nine-thirty," Warren mumbled.

"We'd better get started," Lynn said as she arose. Warren tried to keep his eyes from staring at her figure, full, well formed, and vibrant. As she disappeared into the bathroom, his mind lapsed into a state of confused guilt. Twenty-four hours ago he had left a wife and a career. It might as well have been twenty-four years. He sat up in bed and stared out the window. The red bubble on the top of a boarder patrol car brought him to.

"Lynn!" Warren half whispered through the door. "Cops!"

She opened the door immediately as Warren pointed to the car. She grabbed her skirt and shoes.

"Quick, let's get out of here!"

He pulled himself together as best he could, jamming his shirt into his trousers and grabbing his wallet, passport, and the makeup kit. Their unit was on the far side of the complex; if they could get the car started before the trooper left the office, they had a chance. Lynn made a frantic inspection of the room, and the two fugitives were once more on the run.

The car did not fail them; looking backward Lynn saw no one leave the office. Warren was at the wheel now; without any makeup they resembled bums—a liability, because they could be questioned for work permits. New clothes were the first priority.

An ugly splash of neon came into view a few miles down the road. Mexico was not without shopping centers. Warren turned off the main road and parked, as inconspicuously as possible, among a long row of vehicles. As far as he could tell, they had not been followed.

Professor Fellstrom had never been entirely satisfied with the explanation for the cancellation of the Solar III project. Malfunctions do occur, but repairs should have been successful, or, if not, someone should have had the courtesy to tell him one way or the other. The university had spent considerable funds on the venture. Now, department chairmen and directors were starting to ask questions.

Calls to C. A. Richardson, and Warren Belting resulted in excuses. Professor Fellstrom had no way of knowing that, with Charlie in D.C.

under security, and Warren and Lynn escapees, he was being told the truth. The parties *were* unavailable. Initially Professor Fellstrom wanted to suggest that Solar III might prove useful in documenting the possibility of a loss of solar energy being the cause of the record cold wave affecting the entire nation. His was one of a number of theories proposed in academic circles to explain the phenomena; he had no way of knowing how accurate his conclusion was.

Perhaps out of bitterness, the professor had decided that, somehow, information was being withheld, and Houston knew more of the matter than was being revealed. If he was the victim of a coverup, Professor Fellstrom wanted to know about it. A final report on Solar III was due next month, and as yet he had little of substance to justify a multimillion-dollar effort by his university. Perhaps "Bumper" could help.

8.
Exposé

Senator Bumper Johnson was an old friend of Professor Fellstrom. They had known each other in Korea, and though from vastly different backgrounds, had become friends. Bumper, whose nickname came from skills derived from years spent in pool halls, had come up through the ranks of organized labor. He was tough, firm, and sometimes crude. He had left school after eighth grade to support two younger brothers and an ailing mother. His education had to come from the mills, and unionism became his trade. Bumper had never lost an election, from his first as president of the local union to three successful bids for senator. He knew the secret—find the right issue and run like hell with it. Sitting in his Washington, D.C., office, cursing the bitter cold, Bumper welcomed the ring of his phone.

"Well hello, Professor. How's Mary and the kids? Fine? That's good. Maybe we can get together Thanksgiving, yeah, good. Say, what can I do for you?...You don't say. You think that's got something to do with it? Coverup, eh? They're hiding something? Well, let me do some good ol' checking on that one. Yeah, sure as hell is cold here too; everybody's complaining about it. I'll let you know as soon as I find out something. Sure nice talkin' to you, Professor, and make sure you say hi to Mary and the kids. Thanks. Bye now."

Bumper hung up slowly; Professor Fellstrom had just handed him a hot new issue on a silver platter.

Bumper knew where to start. If there was one son-of-a-bitch who would try and cover up something like this it had to be Weld Smith. He represented Texas oil, Texas oil had put him in his office as Secretary of National Energy Resources, and Texas oil paid his dues, Bumper was convinced. He had never been able to prove anything one way or the other, but, like looking for an outhouse in the dark, you don't have to see it to know where it is. Weld's office and the outhouse had one thing in common: they both stank.

Bumper braced himself against the bitter cold and headed his car across town. It would be better to surprise Weld than to give him advance warning. Bumper knew Weld had some knowledge of the professor's experiment. Weld had praised the project at a hearing as an example of government-civilian cooperation. Best thing to do was to hit Weld hard and fast.

"Wall, hello there, Senator! What brings you out on such a cold day?" Weld was his usual self.

Bumper looked him in the eye. "Solar III, Mister Secretary, Solar III. Know anything about it?" Weld's expression told Bumper he'd hit pay dirt; now for some digging.

"Wall, as you know, Senator, that's one of our cooperative deals with them university profs out there in your terry-tory. Don't reckon I got much to report—somethin' went wrong with it, an' they ain't got it fixed, far as I know."

Bumper sat down and thought for a moment. Then, "Mister Secretary, you don't think your people might know a little more than they're saying about what's causing all this cold weather? A lot of people are going to starve if this keeps up, and some of them might be people who voted me in here, know what I mean?"

Weld's face flushed with anger. "Why, you just sit there an' accuse me of lyin', like you're God hisself. I think, Senator, your welcome is run out!" Weld got up and walked toward the office door.

"I thank you, Mister Secretary," Bumper commented on his way out. "You've been most helpful."

He had his answer now. Weld was in the thick of it. Bumper knew he needed more details before he could move in on the secretary. He'd spend a few days thinking about it. Many a senator had made the fatal error of pointing a finger at the wrong person.

Bumper settled his frame into the friendly old leather chair behind an ancient wooden desk and surveyed the stacks of correspondence that lay unanswered. Almost all of it dealt with the cold weather. When was the federal government going to declare disaster areas or supply emergency aid? Funny, how most voters were more interested in treating the effect rather than solving the cause of a problem. Perhaps it was human nature; you were damned if you did and damned if you didn't.

Bumper packed one of the stacks of letters in his briefcase and turned off the desk light. He stared for a moment at the strange winter scene outside the window. It was beautiful, but so untimely. His mind returned to his constituency, their lost crops, cold homes, and pleas for aid. Time to head for the apartment and answer a few of the letters as best he could.

Bumper had lived alone ever since his wife died of cancer some five years ago, leaving him with two grown children and five grandchildren. He seldom saw any of them; they were spread across the world—Africa to Australia. Bumper worried about them though. How were they doing with the cold? Would they have enough food?

He walked the six blocks through the snow. Children were everywhere, enjoying the rare treat. Bumper could not remember any other snowfall in D.C.—and it wasn't even Thanksgiving yet. He'd cook up some hot chili and coffee before the letters.

The telephone ringing brought Bumper to. He had dozed off in front of the fire, its heat soothing his mind into sleep. He had no idea how long it had been ringing.

"Senator Johnson?" a faint voice asked.

"Yes, this is the senator speaking," Bumper replied.

"My name is Sherri Sokowski. I'm Secretary Smith's receptionist. I need to see you right away." She sounded afraid, Bumper thought. God, Weld Smith's girl calling him. Time for a little caution, Bumper decided.

"Miss Sokowski, what do you wish to see me about?"

There was a pause. "It's in regard to your visit to the Secretary—I'd rather not discuss it over the phone, though."

Bumper decided to take the plunge. "Okay, I'll be here all evening," he replied, "but it's a bad night to be out anywhere."

The voice at the other end sounded anxious. "You will see me tonight—it's very important." Bumper gave her his address and offered to pay the taxi fare. He hung up the receiver slowly. Talk about being out on a limb; he hardly knew the girl. Weld Smith could be setting him up for one dandy fall, yet she might just by chance be acting on her own. Bumper put the coffeepot back on the stove and stoked the fire. One way or another this was going to be one hell of an interesting evening.

"Good evening, Senator." The figure in the doorway was slight, but not fragile. Framed by a scarf, her face was angular, clean, and pretty without the layers of makeup required by most Washington women.

"Come in, come in." Bumper closed the door behind Sherri Sokowski. He hoped he had guessed right on this one, or the career of Senator Johnson could end quickly.

He took her coat and noticed the slim, well-tailored figure. Sherri probably had few clothes, but those she owned were expensive. Her hair was long, black, and neatly parted in the middle.

"Like some coffee, Miss Sherri?" Bumper could hear the pot steaming.

"Yes, thank you very much," she replied, standing by the fire. She was very attractive in the flickering light.

"Senator, after your visit with the secretary today, I felt that I had to tell someone what has been going on." Sherri paused to accept the coffee. "Thanks. Well, this weather thing is going to hurt a lot of people, and I guess we should be helping all we can instead of hiding."

Bumper questioned her. "Hiding, you said?"

"Yes," Sherri continued. "You see, there was a meeting with the people in Houston about a satellite—Solar III, I think. Anyway this satellite somehow has sensed that the sun's heat is decreasing. Nobody knows exactly why, but my boss lied to you when he said he knew nothing."

Bumper looked at her, incredulous. "You mean that all along Weld Smith knew what was going on and has kept it a secret? For Christ sake, why?"

Sherri looked into the fire. "I don't know exactly. He has a friend, an oil man in Texas, Mr. Redding, I believe. He's been giving this

Mr. Redding all of the information about the cold weather. They have some kind of a deal, but I don't know what it is."

Bumper didn't know what to say for a moment. As a professional politician he could not yet believe his ears. He thought Weld Smith was smarter than that, but greed does strange things to a man. There could only be one explanation for Weld's actions. He and Redding were going to profit from oil sales, the dirty bastards.

"Sherri, this is very important." Bumper looked her in the eye. "Are you absolutely certain that what you have told me is true?"

"Yes, Senator." She was calm, almost relieved. "It is the truth, I swear it."

Bumper's mind was in a whirl. She couldn't go back to Weld's office now. Before he could use the information in any way he had to protect her.

"Sherri," Bumper spoke more as a father, "you can't go back there now. No telling what Weld Smith might do to you once he knows the word is out. Before I can do anything we've got to get you into a safe place." She seemed to understand.

"Now listen carefully," Bumper said slowly. "I've got a farm in Vermont where you can stay for a while until this mess blows over. Nobody must know where you are—not even your parents." She nodded.

Bumper continued, "Call in sick tomorrow morning, pack your clothes, and give me a call when you are ready. I'll get you to the bus station, and have your things stored for safekeeping. The farm has a wood stove, and plenty of food stored. You won't be safe in Washington; Weld Smith can be rough."

He watched her reaction. She was amazingly calm.

"Don't worry, Senator, I'll do exactly as you ask. I trust you."

"More coffee?" Bumper asked.

"No, thanks. I'd better be going now. Thanks." She got up slowly, smoothed her skirt, and shook his hand. Her grip was firm, determined.

"I'll call a cab." Bumper reached for the phone. He really believed her. He didn't know exactly why, but he did.

They stood for a moment facing each other, jointly aware that what had been shared between them tonight could not be unshared. They had cast their lot together. Bumper finally spoke.

"A lot of people, including myself, will be grateful for your honesty—perhaps it isn't too late to do something, I hope not." He heard the cab outside. The horn told of an impatient driver. Bumper helped her with her coat; he thanked her again and watched Sherri Sokowski disappear into the night.

Bumper sat for some time staring into the fire, watching the embers die and grow cold. The reality of the events of the evening seeped slowly into his mind. Weld Smith had a reputation for corruption, but this went far beyond simple greed. Every day that information was withheld meant further loss of life and future starvation for the world. Bumper trusted and respected his government. He was hurt and bitterly disappointed in Smith's action. One person should not have that much power to destroy.

Gradually Bumper's thoughts changed to tactics. How should he proceed? His first concern was Sherri; she had to be covered. The farm was a perfect hiding place. No one in Washington, as far as he knew, was aware he owned such a spot, and with food and provisions one could survive a hard winter with a little pluck. A couple of phone calls early tomorrow would do for making arrangements.

The most difficult task would be the news release. He had little factual knowledge other than her disclosure, and he would have to be extremely careful in his handling of Weld Smith. Taking a sheet of paper, he began: "Informed sources have disclosed today that high government officials have known for some time of a major solar disturbance...Indications are that this information concerning the worldwide cold wave has been deliberately withheld from publication by certain individuals seeking private gain." It was a good start.

Bumper slept little that night. He awoke to the sight of frost on the window and more snow. God, he hoped the buses were running. He forced himself to get dressed. The coffeepot was still on the stove from last night. Bumper had difficulty believing that it had all happened, yet there was the draft of his news release on the desk. He dialed the bus depot. The ring went unanswered for some time.

"Hello." Finally. "Central depot."

"Do you have anything going north to Rutland, Vermont?"

"Yessir, one moment." Bumper could hear the rustle of paper. "Eleven-thirty A.M., three connections, get you in Rutland at ten-fifteen tonight. We got some slow-ups due to this weather, though—may be a little later."

"Okay, thanks a lot," Bumper replied, hanging up the receiver. Now for Sherri's call.

He cracked two eggs into the old fry pan and filled the toaster. This was no day to start on an empty stomach. The warmth of the kitchen stove felt good against the chill. He expertly flipped the eggs and grabbed the toast as it popped up, warm and brown. Halfway through his breakfast the phone rang; it was Sherri. She was packed and had called in to her office leaving a message on Secretary Smith's answering-service tape. Bumper told her the bus schedule; he would pick her up at ten-thirty this morning. He also told her to stay in her apartment and not answer any calls. He noted her address and hung up. A lot of work needed to be accomplished between now and ten-thirty.

Bumper called the country store at Centerway, Vermont; he gave Sherri's name as his granddaughter, Mary Johnson, and told them it was okay to give her credit. With all the ski crowd in the area no questions would be asked. Next, he called Mr. Samsick, his caretaker. He would see that there was a good supply of food and fuel at the farm. No telling how long she might have to stay.

Bumper made one final arrangement for holding his news conference. He called the Senate press office and reserved the conference room for four o'clock that afternoon. Bumper went over his draft of the news release and decided to type it himself. He wanted to make certain Sherri was well on her way to safety before anyone other than himself knew of the contents.

Bumper picked up the staff limo at ten and drove to Sherri's address. It was in a neighborhood populated by young singles, mostly secretaries and staff aides—a good life if you were between the ages of twenty and thirty, good looking, and single. Sherri greeted him with a wave from the door. Four well-worn suitcases probably contained her life's possessions. Her belongings were sparse, and Bumper figured he could store them in the basement of his town house without difficulty.

"You still want to go through with it?" he asked her. She nodded affirmatively. He was surprised at how easily she managed two suitcases. He carried the other two and loaded them into the limo. Bumper was glad that he had brought the big car.

The bus station was crowded, with weather delays adding to the confusion. They found a place on one of the long benches in the back waiting room where chances of being seen were slim. Bumper gave her a packet of instructions, some keys, and a copy of the letter of reference.

"Stock the place with plenty of food, now, 'cause no telling how long you might have to stay," he cautioned. "You'll have to draw your own water from the well and heat it on the stove. There's not much in the way of plumbing facilities. either."

"I was raised on a farm in northern Wisconsin," Sherri replied. "I'll get along okay."

Bumper knew, somehow, she would. He looked at his watch.

"Time to go now." He picked up the two heaviest bags, and she followed. The bus, snow covered and showing signs of a hard previous journey, was waiting. Bumper shook her hand firmly.

"Good luck, now, you're doing a brave thing."

She handed him a letter.

"This is for my father. He's in a rest home in Wisconsin. As he is my only living relative, I'd like him to know what I'm doing. Could you mail it for me?"

"Certainly," replied Bumper, "and I'll forward your mail as well. Might even write you myself."

"That would be nice." Sherri meant it. There was something in the makeup of Senator Johnson she admired. He was tough, honest, yet considerate and kindly. Like her father, Bumper seemed automatically to know what to do.

"Good-bye," she called.

"Bye, and good luck now." Bumper waved at the figure in the window. Not all the heroes fought in wars.

Bumper pressed the limo into the traffic, slowed by the snow, and made his way back to the office. He wanted to call Professor Fellstrom before the news conference to alert him and to thank him for the lead. He'd send him a copy of the news release as a followup. On the way into the office building he mailed Sherri's letter to her father. He noticed the address—"Soldiers' Home, Sparta, Wisconsin." He'd have to get out that way sometime to see him.

Bumper's news conferences were never very well attended. His releases were for the most part good news such as military academy appointments and awards to constituents. The media wanted only the scandal, the bad kind of news that sells papers. The more violence, the more people killed, the better. Well, today he'd surprise them.

The conference room was almost empty: a few junior reporters as usual and one lone TV cameraman from a local station. They arose, politely, as he walked to the podium.

"Ladies and gentlemen," Bumper began. He was brief, but he named Secretary Smith and detailed the coverup of the Solar III data. The reporters could hardly believe their ears; they were witness to one of the greatest exposés in recent history, and not one member of any of the major news services was present. They had it to themselves; pandemonium broke loose. Some ran for the phones while others tried to pump Bumper for additional details, to no avail. He would not name his source; he would only say that it was accurate, and confidential. By the end of the conference, several major news media reporters had entered the room.

"You're late, fellas," Bumper commented. "I started at four."

He was mobbed in the hallway, but escaped eventually to the privacy of his office. He took the phone off the receiver to stop the ringing.

Bumper settled into the big leather chair, sighed, and thought for a few minutes. Then he picked up a bill from the stack on the desk. It asked for federal funds to keep the Great Lakes shipping lanes free from ice. The bill had the endorsement of Weld Smith's department. Bumper put it down on the desk and laughed. He laughed until the tears came, and then he cried. God—what a mess.

9.
Refuge

The two figures that emerged from the Mexican clothing store would have passed for any number of American tourists, with their bright shirts and Western jeans topped off with sunglasses and sombreros. Lynn laughed at Warren.

"You look real cute in that get-up."

He was not impressed.

"At least it's warmer and clean," Warren commented as he tossed their old clothes into a refuse can. "Let's get something to eat. I'm starved."

Thinking back, Lynn couldn't remember when they'd had a complete meal.

They parked the old car on a side street and walked to a hotel; the appearance of the car might raise questions. The lobby was full of tourists dressed much like Warren and Lynn. If they stayed with the tourist groups, they were relatively safe. Registering as Mr. and Mrs. W. Downs, they ambled over to the elevator and joined a tour group going up to their floor. They were an odd lot—Mexicans and Americans, students, and elderly couples evidently spending a day in Monterrey before flying to Europe. They were all complaining about the cold weather and unheated tourist buses.

Warren opened the door to their room and collapsed on the bed.

"We've got to plan some strategy, War. Our money won't go far living like tourists. And we've got to get out of Mexico, 'cause sooner or later they'll find us."

"Yeah, I know," Warren replied, "but where the hell to go? If we join one of these groups to Europe, it's going to be a hell of a lot colder over there."

"Let's eat." Lynn changed the subject. "We can buy several international newspapers—maybe we'll see something."

She disappeared into the bathroom to wash up, leaving Warren alone. He had to find work wherever they went; they would need food and shelter if they were going to survive. A rural, smaller town would be better than residing in a large city; rural folk were more independent, and could survive the cold. Cities, he reckoned, would be in a state of chaos once the knowledge of solar dimming was known. Yet work might be difficult to find in a small town.

Lynn emerged, fresh and downright attractive, Warren noticed. She bent over and kissed him. "Lunch time, War. Let's go."

They picked up several international papers and paged through the classified ad sections. Jobs were scarce, mostly seamen, oil drilling riggers, and the like. Not much for couples, particularly fugitives from the U.S.

The lunch was typical tourist fare—charred hamburger, and expensive. Warren was thankful for the good Mexican beer. It served as a wash for the bad food.

"Let's take these papers up to our room and spend some time going through them. There must be something," Lynn suggested.

"Fine. I'll pay for this garbage," Warren replied. They rejoined at the elevator.

"Christ," Warren muttered. "Ten bucks for two hamburgers and a couple of beers."

"I know," Lynn replied. "We'll find something better tonight."

They spent most of the afternoon going over the papers, with little success. One ad did list a local employment agency in Monterrey, and something about a thermoelectric plant in Stongsfjörd, Iceland. One other company in England was looking for coal mining engineers, something Warren knew little about.

"Let's stop at the employment agency, and then look for a better place for dinner. I'd also like to pick up a razor, toothbrushes, and some underwear." Lynn was, as usual, practical, and correct. They had only the clothes they'd purchased that morning, and Warren hadn't shaved for a couple of days.

"Fine," he concurred. "I'm ready."

The agency listed in the paper was located in one of the modern high-rise office buildings that had been constructed in anticipation of a real estate boom that never came. The hallways lacked carpeting, and most of the offices appeared vacant. A hastily executed sign over room 742 designated it as "World Employment Services, Walk In" in English and Spanish. Warren spoke to the immaculate receptionist.

"We saw your ad looking for engineers in Iceland. Can you give us any information?" The receptionist rose, came to attention, and pointed a slender finger armed with a half-inch fingernail toward a cubicle.

"Over there, sir," she said, and sat down, still seemingly at attention. Warren and Lynn walked in the direction indicated and noticed an elderly balding gentleman sitting at a desk devoid of any paper save for a small notepad.

"Your name?"

Warren answered, "Mr. and Mrs. Belting."

He felt he'd best use his correct name, because the passports might be needed. The risk had to be taken.

"You are interested in Stongsfjörd, no?"

"Yes," Warren replied.

"Your background, please." The man spoke as a robot might. Warren gave his general history as a civil engineer and government technician, being careful not to mention the Houston lab. He fortunately had worked for several years as a supervisor for Washington Water and Power and relied on that experience for much of the interview. The interviewer nodded with an occasional "good" or "please explain"; otherwise he was uncommunicative.

Finally he turned from Warren to Lynn.

"You, what do you do?"

Lynn was taken by surprise. "Well, I've been a schoolteacher and technician," was all she could counter.

"Good," commented the interviewer. He wrote something on his notepad in a foreign language and called the receptionist.

"Helga?" He turned to Warren. "You will be given details by my receptionist; please follow her instructions if you wish a position."

Helga fished a file from her desk, marked a few of the pages, and handed a brochure to Warren.

"If you have interest, please return by nine A.M. tomorrow. Otherwise we will cancel you." She again extended the sword-embellished finger, this time toward the door. "Good-bye."

After Warren and Lynn left, they quickly completed their shopping, anxious to return to their hotel to review the brochure offered by the employment agency. Thus far, it was the only offer of assistance they'd had, and they ran the risk of being spotted if they stayed in Monterrey much longer. Remembering the horrible hotel food, Lynn suggested that they eat in one of the small Mexican restaurants.

"I don't think I can take another meal like that lunch," she commented. She grabbed Warren's arm and steered him into a quaint building with "El Grande" over the door. A smaller sign in the window stated, "Good Mexican food, tourists welcome." The place was filling up with the early evening tourists, some already well on their way to a headache tomorrow morning. Booths lined the walls offering security in the dim light. It was too dark to read the Icelandic brochure; it would have to wait until the hotel.

"You like to order?" A pretty waitress stood beside their table.

"Yeah," Warren replied. "Two of those Le Grande specials, and two Carta Blancas."

"Thank you, señor." She disappeared into the dim lights and cigar smoke.

"What did you order?" Lynn asked.

"I don't know. It was on the table card as the special of the day—we'll find out." He relaxed, waiting for the beer and soaking up the warmth of the place. If they were going to Iceland, he'd have to get used to the cold, he thought.

The waitress returned with two beers and two plates heaped with food. At least the place didn't suffer for lack of quantity.

"This sure beats the hotel," Lynn commented.

"Yeah, we'd better enjoy it while we can," Warren said as he looked through the window, now frosted with the cold night air. Few people were on the sidewalks now. They must be in the bars and restaurants out of the chilly air. It was difficult to believe that this was Monterrey, Mexico.

Although the distance was short between the restaurant and the hotel, they were both shaking with the cold as they entered the lobby. The hotel's heating system, not used to the demand, was barely able to maintain a comfortable level.

"I'm for a hot shower," Lynn announced as they entered the room.

"Might warm the place up a bit, too," Warren added. "I'll follow you."

Getting into bed to stay warm, Warren and Lynn began to review the brochure given them by the employment agency. The position was one of a project engineer for the Island Construction Co. thermoelectric plant in the process of construction at Stongsfjörd on the west coast of Iceland. It was designed to convert heat energy derived from underground hot springs into electricity. The two-year contract provided transportation, food, and lodging, plus an attractive salary. A three-week leave was allowed each year, with pay. An enclosed folder contained color photos of the country, rugged, beautiful landscapes and quaint fishing villages not unlike those found along the coast of Maine. An additional contract had been included for Lynn, offering a position as a grade-school teacher for the workers' children.

"Now I know how the sailors felt signing up for a whaling voyage," Warren laughed as he spoke. "We fly direct to Reykjavik on their charter plane, so we wouldn't have to pass through any U.S. customs."

Lynn was, as usual, calculating their route.

"There must be a consulate where we could try to get held once we arrived, though I don't know what chance we have of convincing anyone our story is true."

"We've got to try," Warren urged. "If we fail, at least it sounds like one place where we have a chance of staying warm."

"Speaking of staying warm, I'm going to bed. Let's mull over Iceland in our sleep, and decide tomorrow."

Lynn pulled the covers and bedspread over her as she spoke. Warren switched off the light and stared out the window for a while. A fine, light snow was falling. It was an impossible scene for Monterrey, Mexico, yet it was happening. The streets were empty now except for a few taxicabs transporting tourists who were brave enough, or drunk enough, to fight the weather. What would things be like a week, or a month from now? How long could they survive as fugitives, let alone adding the risks associated with the weather? Iceland was a long way to run, but at the moment there was no other option. He turned and slipped beneath the covers, eagerly pulling Lynn close to him. His thoughts and worries dimmed.

The deep red sun was streaming in the room through the window when they awoke. The remains of the wet snowfall were still in evidence, with slush in the streets and dirty gray piles on the sidewalks where shopkeepers had made an attempt to clear their storefronts.

As Lynn was dressing, she commented, "I wish we had a little more choice of clothes; the Western slacks are getting a little old." She looked at Warren, "Well, War, what do we do?"

"Not much question," he replied with a yawn. "We take them up on their offer."

She seemed relieved that Warren had made the decision. Now, at least, they had the chance to survive without detection. There was little doubt in both their minds that, unless they left Mexico, they would eventually be apprehended by U.S. authorities.

They signed the contracts at the employment office that morning and were told to be at Universal Air Charters by eleven that evening. If they missed this flight, the next plane wouldn't leave for two weeks. They would be there.

Most of the day was spent in preparation, shopping for additional clothing and supplies. A list had been provided, along with a weight restriction of fifty pounds for each person. Warren and Lynn returned to the hotel room late that afternoon, and, using the bathroom scale, checked their newly acquired luggage. The shopping trip had cost more than six hundred dollars. The only items they lacked were in the line of insulated, cold-weather clothing. Monterrey, until recently, was no market for such things as parkas and insulated boots.

"I hope we'll have some time to shop in Reykjavik." Lynn looked at the lightweight jackets as she spoke.

They watched the sunset from their window, the last one they would see on the North American continent. The couple well understood their decision; there was no returning now.

They returned to the El Grande for supper since the food had been good and reasonably priced. Tonight, it was not as crowded; the cold weather was having its effect on the tourist business. Warren and Lynn ate slowly, as if it were their last supper. It would be for some time.

Lost in thought, they almost missed the border patrol car parked in front of the hotel. Lynn spotted it first.

"War, they're checking!"

"Christ you're right. Get back over here." He motioned to a store entryway.

"Look." Warren was planning as he was speaking. "Wear your dark glasses and go back to the El Grande. I'll go up the stairway and get our luggage. The contracts are there also. Christ, we've got to have them."

Lynn understood; she squeezed his hand in confirmation.

"Be careful, War." She let go and was off into the dusk.

Warren moved through the hotel bar to avoid the lobby. Two rangers were engaged in conversation with the clerk. They may not have been after them, but the chance could not be taken. He crossed the rear of the lobby and reached the door to the stairs without detection. At the room floor, the hall was vacant. Unlocking the room, he stuffed the contracts into one of the suitcases, slammed both of them shut, and ran for the stairway, closing the room door on his way out.

Looking back, Warren noticed the elevator door open; it was the clerk and the rangers. He watched in horror for an instant as they made their way down the hall toward the room Warren had vacated a moment earlier.

He regained his composure and made his way quietly down the stairs and out through a rear exit. His hands were trembling. He took the back alley to avoid the hotel front and ducked into the restaurant. There was no one on the street as best he could see. Placing the two suitcases beside the coat rack, Warren searched the dim interior for Lynn. A brief wave of panic struck as at first he could not see her. He then saw her face, half hidden, in a booth.

"Oh, thank God." Lynn jumped up and hugged him. "What happened, War?"

He relayed the incidents of the past half hour, including the escape.

"I think we'd better call a taxi and get out to the airport, even though it's early," he concluded.

A strange mixture of people were assembled at Universal Air Charters that evening when Warren and Lynn arrived. One tour group was obviously made up of college students taking advantage of the low overseas air fare. Their group was an international mixture, recruited from campuses of the world. What a job it would be overcoming the language barrier. A century ago they would have made up a fine crew bound to chase Moby Dick; today their trip would become an adventure of survival.

The attendant checked their travel vouchers and passports. He gave them hardly a second glance as Warren and Lynn joined the others in the small, crowded waiting room.

The couple next to them, conversing in German, were obviously quite excited about the trip. They had acquired a small map of Iceland and were trying to locate Stongsfjörd. Across from them sat a Japanese couple, quietly waiting. A number of children, utilizing the universal language of play, were laughing and running around a row of seats engaged in a variation of the old game of musical chairs. Various pieces of luggage were scattered about the room, along with an assortment of clothing.

How many of these people, Warren wondered, were fugitives like them, escaping one life for another. Had it not been for the secret they shared, Warren almost might have enjoyed the adventure. He tried to identify the various people in their group with professions; most were no doubt technical. Such a project would require a number of disciplines, and the language of the technical world is universal.

Warren's mind returned to his own plight, one career lost and another about to begin. Career hell, he had thrown away his entire past life. His home, Sally, the good lifestyle of upper-middle-class Houston, Texas, were all a matter of past record. He was in a strange country living with a stranger, and now among strangers from around the world. Being a fugitive had limited the options. One could not enjoy the luxury of choice with the Texas Rangers, border patrol, and the FBI, to name a few, at their heels. They were damn lucky to find this chance.

The announcement of the flight interrupted Warren's thoughts. He squeezed Lynn's hand, and they made their way down a long corridor to a small departure gate. Beyond, the dim outline of a vintage commercial jet was visible. It had been reprinted with "Universal Air Charters" lettering the length of the fuselage, though the tail still bore the well known colors of a major U.S. commercial airline.

"Well, here goes nothin'," Warren quipped as he and Lynn mounted the stairs to the cabin. A steward showed them to their seats, and jammed their luggage into a compartment that had at one time been the first-class galley. The seats were worn, with the upholstery torn and soiled.

"Gosh, I hope the engines are in better shape than the seats." Lynn's voice showed her nervousness. The steward checked all their passports and gave takeoff instructions in six languages as the cabin lights flickered with the starting of the engines. Warren reclined his seat and closed his eyes, exhausted from the evening's events. The life of a fugitive was a tiring one. He felt the wheels grow light, then leave the runway. Lynn's head was on his shoulder.

10.
Ice

The cabin was quiet, with most of the passengers trying to catch some sleep. The dawn would come early as the flight moved east and north. Below, the ocean lay still, cold, with the beaches of the Gulf Coast deserted. Warren found a blanket in the compartment over the seat and covered himself and Lynn. The drone of the jet engines lulled him to sleep.

"Look, War. Look at all that ice and snow." It was Lynn shaking him. They were passing over the southern tip of Greenland, the dawn casting red hues across the vast, frozen emptiness.

"I hope Iceland isn't like that," Warren added. "If it is, we've come to the wrong part of the world to survive this thing."

They watched as the land disappeared and the ocean, now filled with ice floes, again dominated the scene.

The steward was serving hot coffee and cold rolls, evidently Universal Air Charters' breakfast fare. It was better than nothing. The cabin was returning to life with the procession of passengers to the washrooms and the voices of the children. Lynn got up to join the line. Warren found an old magazine in the seat pocket and tried to concentrate on reading; it was no use. In spite of it all he found himself excited. The fear of capture had lessened with distance, and the chance for survival had improved. Warren was amazed at how remote Houston, Texas, seemed. His leaving Sally had not been the traumatic experience he had visualized. It was as if a long trip had intervened and a natural new life easily evolved. He began to doubt if Sally would welcome him back if he did return. She had not believed his story before he left; she certainly would not believe it now.

"God, what a mob for one washroom." Lynn had returned from the line looking better. She had a way of bouncing back from an ordeal.

She watched the ocean from the window, anticipating the first sight of Iceland. She hadn't long to wait. The island was soon visible, accompanied by the sound of the pilot's voice.

"We will be landing shortly at Reykjavik International Airport. Please fasten your seat belts, and extinguish smoking materials." Again, the multinational announcement.

The snow cover was lighter than they had expected, with patches of bare, exposed ground visible. The runway was clear. A bright sun welcomed them as the plane touched down. They had arrived.

The group was met by a customs official who was principally concerned with cigarettes and liquor. The weather was cold, but somehow not as bitter as Monterrey. Perhaps the warm ocean currents moderated the climate. Suitcases were piled high on the top of an airport bus, and they started up the coast to Iceland's largest city, Reykjavik. The driver announced that they would have three hours in the city before proceeding to Stongsfjörd.

"Great," Lynn smiled. "We'll have time to buy some good Icelandic clothes." Their Mexican tourist garb was hardly the thing for this climate.

Wool clothing proved to be inexpensive, well made, and unbelievably warm. Lined boots and jackets finished out a basic wardrobe that was to prove vital to their survival. Lynn purchased one wool suit, "just in case" a chance to dress up occurred.

They returned to the bus to find that most of the group had done as they had. The driver urged them aboard and advised them that Stongsfjörd was five hours to the North. They wished that there had been more time to enjoy Reykjavik, for the city had all the charm of a Scandinavian seaport. Scattered among the traditional buildings were a few modern high-rise hotel and office structures. Many of the homes were surrounded by courtyards, and all had red metal roofs. Flowers and lace curtains graced the windows. Wooden window frames were often painted in bright contrasting colors with the rest of the home. The city and the air were clean and fresh beyond description. Since the entire city derived its heat from hot springs, there was no need to burn coal or oil.

The city disappeared behind them as the bus headed north along the coast. The landscape was barren but beautiful, with mountains and crystal-clear streams everywhere. A few small farms dotted the valleys, red roofs outlined by the snow-covered fields. The road was unpaved, and snow-packed from use. It was difficult to tell if the country had been affected by the cold. The streets of Reykjavik had been considerably more crowded than those of Monterrey. Perhaps the inhabitants were just used to it here.

The trip took most of the day with but one stop for a lunch consisting of fish and lamb sandwiches and a choice of coffee or milk. Large chocolate bars were distributed for dessert, quite a hit among the children. Due to the latitude and time of year, the sun barely rose above the horizon, making sightseeing limited. Warren and Lynn wished that they could have seen more of the country. Unspoiled beauty was a treat to the Americans, used as they were to billboards, litter, and other types of assorted highway blight.

It was dark when they arrived at the Stongsfjörd thermal site. Long rows of modular housing units stood stark against the snow, with hastily erected streetlights casting an eerie, pale-green glow over the landscape. Beyond the encampment, the outline of several large buildings loomed, evidently half-completed generator and transmission units. The site area appeared to be a large valley with steep mountains on either side, and a large river, or fjord, at the lower end.

"Home sweet home, hon," Lynn smiled. She was anxious, as was Warren, to stop running for a spell and rest.

They gathered their luggage and were directed into a large structure obviously used for a combination dining, meeting and recreation hall. Rows of tables and chairs filled half the room, with a lounge, small bar, television, and movie screen occupying the remainder of the space. Bookcases along one wall were filled with books, records, and magazines—the extent, evidently, of cultural assets at Stongsfjörd. The aroma of food cooking filled the air.

A man appeared in the front of the room and, using a portable microphone, asked for attention first in English, then in several other languages. Lodging assignments would be given after the meal; all units were of uniform quality, and there would be a general meeting for all those assigned work contracts at 9:00 P.M.

"That includes us." Warren was anxious to learn his new profession.

Lynn was more interested in the operation. "I wonder who is running this show?" she questioned.

"Still reminds me of the army," Warren replied.

The ringing of a bell signalled dinner, and the group began to sit down at the tables. Warren and Lynn were joined by three couples of Oriental descent.

"You American?" one of the men asked. It was the first time Warren and Lynn had been with anyone since their escape. Half afraid, Warren answered, "yes." The answer was greeted with smiles and the universal "Ah so!"

Trays of food interrupted the brief conversation. The meal was one to become common in the months ahead: flat bread, cheese, boiled fish and butter sauce, boiled potatoes, milk, steaming hot coffee, and fruit soup for dessert. Although slightly foreign in taste, the meal was delicious and left Warren and Lynn feeling relaxed and a little sleepy.

"I hope I can stay awake till nine," Lynn murmured. The food had affected others in a similar fashion; heads were nodding at some of the other tables. Several couples were inspecting the library while sipping cups of hot, black coffee.

True to the earlier promise, room assignments were given everyone after the meal. The basic living unit consisted of a small living room, kitchenette, bath, and one or two bedrooms. Each individual was given a key and a map with the unit-number location shown. Some of the group, wives and children who did not have to stay for the meeting, left immediately to inspect their new homes.

Lynn and Warren busied themselves reading the map and brochure. The town was complete within itself, including a small commissary, church, hospital, and indoor recreation hall. A bus terminal was the assembly point for transportation to and from the work sites.

"Not quite as spread out as Houston," Lynn laughed. "Houston." The name, to Warren, seemed years in the past. But for the present, there was no looking backward. Survival, day by day, was the only thing that mattered.

The introductory meeting took over an hour, because several languages were required. The project, jointly sponsored by Iceland and Norway, was one to develop energy from the Stongsfjörd thermal area, energy for powering an oil refinery supplied with crude oil from the North Sea fields. Eons ago an earthquake had formed an underground fault, allowing seawater to contact hot lava flows. For years steam thus generated had seeped to the surface and had been tapped for heating greenhouses. Massive deep wells had now been completed, allowing equally massive amounts of steam to be drawn off for power generation. The supply was constantly renewed by the underground flow of seawater, resulting in an almost unlimited source of power. An added bonus was that the seawater in the fjord was also warmed sufficiently to prevent ice formation, thus providing an all-weather deep-water port for the tankers. Fishing boats also took advantage of the resource, accounting for the fresh fish on the menu.

Lynn nudged Warren. "If there was ever a perfect chance for survival, this has got to be it!"

"Yeah, I think you're right. Just as long as the feds don't catch up with us."

"Shhh!" Lynn cautioned. For the present, at least, one couldn't be too careful.

The session finished with some slides of the construction site and artistic renditions of the completed project. The effort would take five years in addition to the first year's work that was already finished.

Job assignments were based on employee tests given in the Mexican office. Warren was assigned supervision of the power control system while Lynn would be teaching grades one through seven in the style of the old one-room country school.

"I think you got the better deal," she commented. "That's an awful spread of kids."

"At least we'll both be inside for the most part though," Warren added. "I can't see my Texas blood getting used to this kind of weather."

After receiving detailed instructions as to where to report to work, and where to obtain any more necessary clothing, Lynn and Warren made their way to unit seventy-six—their "new" home. Opening the door, they were almost overcome by the heat.

"Christ, how do you turn this thing down." Warren cursed as he first found the light switch and then the valve on the single large steam radiator, evidently sufficient to heat a dwelling several times the size of this unit. The room was simply decorated with carpeted floors, curtained windows, and a modern American television set. The bed was made up with a deep, lightweight eiderdown. The bath had a large tub and shower with the added feature of a steam-heated floor. The kitchenette was minimal, but sufficient for the light cooking they'd do, since the main food service was provided.

"It's late, hon," Lynn said as she started to undress. "We start tomorrow at six. I'm for that nice shower and bed."

Warren watched her. Tired as he was, the sight of her figure warmed him. He lay down on the bed and watched her disappear into the bathroom. Tonight they were free, undiscovered, and the rest of the world, as far as he was concerned, could go straight to hell.

Hot water was no problem if the clouds of steam issuing from the bathroom were any indication of supply.

"I've decided I like Iceland," Lynn announced as she emerged from the shower wrapped in a towel. Her skin was bright and glowing from the heat. Warren repeated the process and let the rigors of the day work out as his body soaked up the moist heat.

Reluctantly, he shut off the water and dried himself off. Turning out the light, he pulled the quilt over him and felt Lynn's body, still warm from the shower, next to him. She hugged him, and his last thoughts were of drifting off to sleep in her arms.

The alarm awoke them in what seemed the dead of night. It was 5:00 A.M., and first breakfast was at 5:30.

Small wonder they had seen few other people when they arrived the night before. They were probably all asleep!

They dressed and put on the warm jackets and boots issued to them the night before. The equipment was definitely made for Arctic use.

The dining hall was crowded this morning with the existing residents mixing with the newcomers. It was a surprisingly jovial group, considering the hour. Breakfast consisted of hot cereal, eggs, sausage, cheese, fruit, dry toast, and rolls, along with the usual steaming cups of coffee. Conversation was limited that morning because their breakfast companions were German and knew virtually no English. Smiles and nods of heads sufficed.

The bus terminal had the work sites numbered. Matching the proper number with your instruction card hopefully got you off in the proper direction. For the first time, Lynn and Warren had to separate; they squeezed hands for a moment and then parted.

Warren's work site was the main power station office and distribution center. Here, eventually all the generating equipment would be monitored and the electricity transmitted by power line down to the refinery. His background in rocket and satellite systems was a real asset. It was only a short time before he felt at home and, except for the language barrier, found himself directing the tasks with little effort.

For the first time, too, he had a real chance to survey the weather conditions. It was colder than usual for this time of year, and there had evidently been heavier snowfall than forecast. But the effect of solar dimming was more noticeable nearer the equator for some unknown reason. Perhaps the usual lack of sunlight at this time of year diminished the effect; at any rate, no one was visibly concerned about weather conditions.

Lynn found the school well equipped but somewhat confining. The teaching aids used were as up-to-date as in any comparable school in the U.S. Twenty-eight students were enrolled in the English-speaking section. Some were newcomers like Lynn, but most had been on the "island" for the duration of the project—about two years as far as Lynn could discern.

Teaching was quite a change for her. She had been used to working with adults and machines. Conversing with the younger children, particularly, was difficult to adjust to. Nonetheless Lynn found herself enjoying the work. Most of the students were bright and eager to learn. Several asked questions as to her past and Lynn was cautious, only saying that she was from the western U.S. and had taught school in a small town. Enough said.

Evenings were spent in the library section of the dining hall reading or watching television. Many of the U.S. programs were aired over the Icelandic network, and news programs, although in Icelandic, carried English subtitles. Warren usually watched the late news to determine if anything had happened since their departure. Weather was certainly in the news, but was treated mainly as an "unexplained cold wave." Tourism in Florida and other southern resort areas had been severely affected, and government officials were predicting fuel shortages and higher food prices. How long would they sit on it? he wondered. Probably until they were forced in some fashion to reveal the truth. Next year was an election year and bad news had a way of being withheld by the incumbents. But these questions were soon to be answered.

They'd been on the island about a week and Warren was in the library one evening half asleep waiting for the news. Lynn had returned to their quarters to prepare for her classes. She seemed to enjoy this life; if anything, she adapted more easily to change than Warren. He missed the Houston lifestyle—the responsibility and excitement of his work there and the easy living. Yet he had certainly found something in his relationship with Lynn that had been missing in his marriage. He enjoyed being with her; she made him feel at home, even in this place. Sally had always accepted him, but little beyond that. She was a china doll and played the role.

The news returned his mind to Stongsfjörd. After the usual world wrap-up, there was a special report from Washington D.C. Warren couldn't believe it—a Senator Johnson had charged the administration with withholding information received from a satellite that the energy from the sun was decreasing at an alarming rate, and that the recent worldwide cold wave was a direct result. Named in the plot were Secretary Weld Smith and a Texas oilman. The information had been withheld, charged Senator Johnson, in an attempt to recoup windfall profits from increased demand for petroleum products. Houston space-center officials were to be questioned by a congressional panel. Two technicians believed to be involved had escaped to Mexico.

"Christ, they know the whole goddam thing." Warren was shaking; he had to get out of there. He got up slowly and went over to the bar; there was little concern among the viewers. Another U.S. scandal meant little to the group in Iceland.

The bartender was an Australian. He winked at Warren. "You blokes got another stink goin, eh?"

"Yeah, I guess so." Warren tried to be casual in his reply. He gulped down a beer. "Think I'll call it a night," he announced.

"G'night, yank," the bartender replied. Warren donned his heavy jacket and walked slowly to the exit. Once outside he ran the full distance to their quarters. He burst in on Lynn, who was curled up in her bathrobe reading. He pulled her out of the chair.

"It's out! It's all over! It was on the TV!" She looked at him in amazement.

"Calm down, War. What in the world do you mean?"

He told her of the news report and of the fact that they were wanted for the investigation.

"Christ, what will we do?" he asked of her.

Lynn waited a moment, then replied slowly, "Nothing. Nothing at all. We stick it out right here." She was correct. No one knew them here, and the government would be hard pressed to trace their route. Theirs was the last group to be retained, so the Monterrey Employment Office was probably closed. They were safe unless someone here made the connection.

"I think I'll grow a beard," Warren quipped.

She smiled and kissed him. "I'll still love you anyway." Soon the lights were out in unit seventy-six and the Icelandic night took over at Stongs.

11. Critique

Washington D.C. had been anything but quiet since Bumper Johnson's press conference when he had charged Weld Smith with the responsibility for withholding evidence on Solar III. Indeed, blame fixing was in full swing. As usual, before any attempt at a solution was started, blame for the incident had to be placed on one of the political parties.

Bumper had received the expected threatening phone call from Weld; he had connected Sherri with the leak and had told Bumper that "if I ever get my hands on that bitch I'll kill her." Sherri was safe for the moment, however, as Weld Smith was under indictment by a federal grand jury. Bumper found himself uncomfortably the public hero of the matter. He was not of an age or mind to capitalize on the circumstance. Rather, he wished the government would realize the implications of the phenomenon and do something to assure an adequate energy and food supply. But many people felt that the whole scheme was a hoax designed to assure higher prices for fuel and groceries.

Meanwhile the weather stayed cold and became colder and, with the change, came belief, then panic. Church attendance was on the increase nationally as well as the suicide rate. A crisis had not developed as yet; it seemed one would have to develop before any effective federal action was initiated. The government was most effective during a crisis, or war; it was as if a certain number of people had to die to create action.

The first group to protest was the farmers' organizations. They had lost a portion of the fall harvest, and the southern citrus crop was almost totally ruined. Feed prices were soaring and, with the federal price control on meat, many ranchers filed bankruptcy. Bumper's mail and telephone calls foretold the coming disaster all too clearly. Yet there was little that Bumper could do in the coming weeks except answer letters and appear at the congressional hearings.

Weld Smith's activities had done little to enhance the position of big oil. Indeed, to many, suspicions were confirmed as to the connection between the government and the petroleum producers. How many were involved was not the question; they were all involved by implication. In the testimony, both Charlie Richardson and Dr. Olsson were exonerated; they had done nothing except report their findings. Charlie had told the investigation that, as far as he knew, Lynn and Warren had disappeared out of fear of being blamed for something not of their doing. The explanation was accepted, something that Lynn and Warren would never know.

For Secretary Smith and Wallace C. Redding of Petroleum International Properties, the matter was quite different. Both were the subject of days of questioning, but little was gained other than the political satisfaction of finding those who were to blame and affixing a suitable punishment. Smith and Redding, as they became known, had been partners in a number of deals involving government kickbacks. The actual dollar figure would never be known; however, both of their careers were finished as a result of Solar III. Both would eventually see prison terms.

The President, although hard pressed for a statement, had kept his silence during the entire investigation, issuing only a brief news release through his press secretary assuring the public that there would be a full investigation and that justice would be done. Although several attempts were made to prove his involvement, none were successful, and other than a tarnished secretary, little damage was done politically. Few looked to the President for any realistic solutions. The office was not designed for such. It was a forthcoming election year and certainly no time for definitive action, other than securing or maintaining the office. The answers, if any, would have to come from the people.

The issue had one positive aspect. For once the United Nations had something of substance to debate. Food, already in critical supply in many lesser developed countries, was now becoming very scarce. And with shortened growing seasons, the prospect was grim worldwide. The fishing industry, generally depressed, was enjoying a worldwide boom. Commercial fishermen, used to working in adverse weather conditions, continued to harvest and receive record prices for their catch. A world surviving on fish was one of the few alternatives.

Human suffering from the cold weather was immeasurable, and much U.N. debate centered on shelter. For many there would be none, and for this winter there were those faced with the choice of freezing or starving to death. The U.N. had suggested a world "food pool" whereby those nations with a surplus supply of food would donate to the less fortunate nations. But faced with the unknown prospect of supply, no nation was willing to give any amount regardless of availability. Thus the problem was stalemated; some would starve sooner than others.

Faced with an angry constituency, Congress had to react, especially in response to the farm bloc. Bumper was appointed to chair a committee whose responsibility it was to recommend emergency legislation. Christmas recess was upon them, and the first meeting was deferred until after the holidays. Bumper had one problem to resolve: Sherri was at the farm awaiting his instructions and something had to be resolved. He felt personally responsible for her safety; she could not return to D.C. until Weld Smith was behind bars, yet the question of food availability concerned him. He decided to spend Christmas at the farm for the first time in many years.

Bumper purchased as many food staples as the station wagon would hold; already shelves in the supermarkets were showing the signs of scarcity. Many items were sold out. Shoppers were buying more as well; they too were becoming afraid of the future.

He called Mrs. Boardman at the Vermont country store. She and her son John had been running the operation since the death of her husband some years ago. She told him that all was well at the farm, and they enjoyed "Mary." John was looking after her, and although the snow had been heavier than usual, they had not suffered.

She was pleased to hear of his plans. It had been many years since that old house had known the joy of a Christmas. He too needed the change and some rest; the recent events would have tired a man many years younger. Perhaps the new year would bring some answers.

The night was cold and clear as he made his way north from D.C., and the roads were free of traffic once the D.C. metropolitan area was behind him. Bumper had filled the car with food and as an added precaution had strapped a full five-gallon can of gasoline to the luggage rack. It would be past midnight before he reached the farm, and gasoline stations were few and far between on the Vermont back country roads. How many times had he driven the route? Through the years, the farmhouse had become a part of him—his joys and sorrows were within its walls. Those who said that a house was without a soul were wrong.

The driveway to the house had been cleared and the walkways neatly shoveled. Someone had put some effort into that task. The porch light came on as he drove up. Sherri was at the door.

"Welcome home, Senator." She gave Bumper a warm hug and took his coat. "There's a fire and hot coffee in the parlor for you."

"Thanks," Bumper replied. He settled himself by the fireplace. The room had been decorated for Christmas, complete with a freshly cut tree trimmed with popcorn garlands and assorted handmade ornaments. The warmth of the fire filled the room—it felt like Christmas as it had been many years ago.

"Here's your coffee, Senator." Sherri was in front of him. She had changed, her eyes sparkled, and there was a lightness in her voice. Bumper sipped the coffee and warmed his feet against the hearth; he could have slept right there for the rest of the night.

Sherri returned from the kitchen. "More coffee?"

"No thanks," he replied.

She smiled. "Your bed is ready and there is a fire in the stove. The water in the pot on the stove should be hot enough for washing by now."

He thanked her and made his way up the stairs, the walnut rail polished from years of use. The bed was turned down, the soft glow of the kerosene lamp filled the room, and the pot simmered on the stove top. A few days of this treatment and he'd be useless in D.C. Bumper washed, banked the fire for the night, and climbed into the old bed. Beneath the quilts he slept, at peace.

It was midmorning when he awoke to voices downstairs and the smell of breakfast cooking. John and his mother had arrived and Christmas Eve preparations were in full swing. Bumper shaved using the water left on the stove, still warm from a well-banked fire, and put on his "Vermont" clothes. D.C. seemed far off indeed.

"Good morning, Senator. Welcome back!" Mrs. Boardman's cheerful voice came from the kitchen where she stood by the massive old wood stove. "Coffee's hot and cakes'll be ready in a jiff."

Bumper felt sorry for those who had never tasted the fare prepared by Mrs. Boardman and that wonderful old stove. He noticed John and Sherri sitting together at one end of the oak kitchen table. Sherri had made friends fast; in fact they both seemed oblivious to anything else in the kitchen.

Bumper smiled at Mrs. Boardman. "Looks like those two are hitting it off all right."

"Mind your own business, Bump," she quipped. "Here's some decent food for you."

Bumper always ate more than he should in Vermont. What a change it was from the usual restaurant stuff in D.C.! "Rubber chicken" was what he called it, and most of it did indeed taste like rubber. He lost track of the number of pancakes that appeared before him as if by magic.

Christmas Eve was always something special at the farm, and this year had a special significance. Unlike so many in the world, they were warm, comfortable, and well fed. A future of cold and starvation was a long way off, or so it seemed.

The small church was crowded full with the townspeople and neighboring farmers. For the moment, fears were put aside and the joy of Christmas reigned. Each individual brought their tithe and placed it before the manger, a custom dating back to the Revolutionary War. Afterward, there were the hymns of Christmas followed by the ringing of the bells. In the candlelight Bumper noticed two figures kiss briefly; it was John and Sherri. New life, rebirth, that's what it was all about, Bumper thought.

Mrs. Boardman stopped him on the way out. "It's just fine, Bump; we know all about her. Won't tell a soul, though. She's a brave one, you know." Bumper felt ashamed at his deceit—he should have known that he could have trusted the Boardmans.

"I'm sorry for the lie," he replied. "You've done wonders for both of us."

Mrs. Boardman put her arm around Bumper. "Merry Christmas, Bump! God bless."

Bumper disliked returning to D.C. after the holidays; the legislative mood was ugly, resentful. Spot food shortages were starting to occur. And the general public was at once blaming the government and asking it for a solution. For the moment, no solution existed, though a number of long-range schemes had been proposed, ranging from atomic-reactor-heated greenhouses to living deep underground to avoid the cold. Meanwhile, the weather got colder.

Worldwide, the effects of the cooling were most severely felt in the tropics, where little or no provisions were made for freezing temperatures. The effect of frost on a jungle is disastrous; leaves wither and die, and with them the animals who rely on such fauna for food. Likewise the native populations were starving. One could only guess at the numbers already lost.

The news media played heavily on the hardships of others, bringing details of worldwide starvation into homes across the U.S. Bitterness, followed by fear, was the logical result.

With Weld Smith under indictment, the full burden of the disaster had fallen on Dr. Gustav Olsson. If there was any chance of a solution, his office was the only hope. The burden weighed on Gus as he flew over central Florida surveying what was once a thriving citrus industry. The trees stood gaunt against the landscape, their leaves fallen, frozen on the ground. These were trees that would never bear fruit again. Yesterday it had been the sugar-cane crop in Louisiana, tomorrow it would be cotton fields in Alabama. They were all dead, and with them the fortunes of their owners.

Gus had released all of the surplus food available. With rationing, the country could survive this winter. If the cold continued, there would be no food surplus next winter—perhaps no new crops at all. How much we took for granted—that the sun would always be there to provide energy. *The sun has betrayed us,* Gus thought.

Dr. Olsson's plane prepared to land at the Florida space center. He was to attend a meeting of the nation's best scientific minds to explore possible solutions to the crisis. A light snow was falling as the plane came to a halt. Gus exited into the cold and quickly sought refuge in a waiting limousine. Other than a few cameramen, the airfield was deserted. The snow continued to fall.

Gus joined the other members of the elite scientific community in the large conference room. During the space exploration era, the room had been used for press and television coverage. Once again, the cameramen had assembled, this time to record an event in the whole earth's struggle for life. Slowly the group assembled around the large, circular table; Gus noticed that Charlie Richardson was among those attending. He moved over to speak to him.

"Hi Charlie. Good to see you."

Charlie's reply barely hinted at the bitterness he still felt from being accused in the conspiracy.

"Oh, hello, Dr. Olsson. Welcome to the sunny South and the Solar III polar bears' club."

"I'm sorry about that," Gus replied. "There was not much any of us could do until they got Weld; he had our hands tied."

Charlie nodded. "Yeah, I suppose so. Got any ideas how to get out of this jam?"

"No, I'm afraid I don't at the moment, Charlie. It looks pretty grim."

The call to order interrupted their conversation. The introductory remarks were quite candid—evidently in an effort to offset the bad publicity generated by the coverup. The sun's energy was reported still decreasing, with the projection that there would be no growing season anywhere in the world by April or May. The world would have to survive on its present food reserves, estimated to be enough for six to nine months. If the solar dimming extended beyond that time, there would be little chance for survival. The news cameras ground on.

A geologist presented data showing the advance of all major glaciers. The advance was increasing at a rate faster than at any time in recorded history. The onset of another ice age was a distinct possibility. *Is this how the last ice age started?* wondered Gus. *Yet early man survived at least one ice age. But there were considerably fewer mouths to feed during that period. How will we feed the present population? How many will die?*

As if to emphasize the need for conservation, lunch consisted only of sandwiches and milk or coffee. It was probably the most primitive meal ever served to such a prestigious group.

The afternoon session was devoted to possible solutions—few existed and fewer were presented. The only ready available mass source of energy was coal, for it would take years to build up enough nuclear energy capacity. Coal could be used to provide thermal energy capable of heating giant, plastic-covered greenhouses. A related idea was to allocate coal to cities where auditoriums and covered sports centers could also be utilized for food propagation. Controls were suggested to restrict excess harvesting of seafood in an effort to extend the availability of that resource. The group effort concentrated on immediate needs, because for some, already starving, the next meal was too late.

Gus felt relieved after the conference. He disliked massive committee efforts, particularly in full view of the television media. Yet the people had a right to know their fate. He slept during most of the return flight to D.C. He was mentally exhausted from the effort. The conference had been held at the suggestion of the President, and the political propaganda implications were obvious, yet Gus was certain that basically the President was concerned. National starvation was hardly a partisan issue. An election year and the key issue was food; for once the politicians had a real gut issue.

The approach of the conference might succeed, for conservation and the massive effort to use coal for thermal crop propagation made sense. Yet one thing had been overlooked—panic, the reaction of a mass of people exposed to terminal starvation. Panic is hard to predict and impossible to control; it often has as its start a single incident such as a televised newscast.

As Dr. Olsson's plane touched down at D.C., some first small incidents had already begun. A food market warehouse in Chicago had been raided, a cold storage locker in Seattle stripped, a corn bin in Kansas emptied of its contents. They were isolated incidents, but the start of the wave. Unaware of anything but the cold, Gus caught a cab home. It was late and tomorrow was another day of unanswered questions.

12.
Panic

If one were to ask where it all began, the Chicago incident would suffice. It was spontaneous panic, though an insignificant incident in itself.

The Chicago-based food chain Midwestern Produce had a large regional warehouse located in a transitional neighborhood on the west side of the city. Filled with supplies for the supermarket members of the chain, it represented a potential source of food for those unable, or unwilling, to pay the current retail prices. For most who took part in the raid, this was their first dishonest act. Perhaps the news coverage of the Florida conference changed their attitudes. Nine months' world food supply is not a great quantity.

The incident started in a small way. A passerby, forever to remain unknown, noticed that a side door had been left ajar. Entering, he noticed the stacked cases of canned produce goods. They would never miss a few; soon his station wagon was full. He sped away. Unloading at home, he was spotted by a neighbor, who was sworn to secrecy in exchange for a case of canned ham. Soon another car pulled up in front of the side entrance to the warehouse, then another. The secret was out.

The police were first called to direct traffic. The source of the activity was unknown to them for some time. The lines of cars lengthened, now including pickups and small trucks. Many were loaded with cases of food. The call went out for assistance. Some store or warehouse was the scene of a mass robbery. Unable to make any headway through the traffic, a helicopter was dispatched to locate the scene. The officers could not believe what they saw; the warehouse was surrounded by thousands of people and cars. Shopping carts and even bicycles had been pushed into service.

In an effort to halt the mass looting, several policemen were lowered onto the warehouse roof. Using loudspeakers, they attempted to quell what now was developing into a full-scale riot. It was doubtful if anyone heard them. The police then fired a few shots, which proved to be a fatal mistake. The response was a fusillade of bullets from the crowd. One policeman lay dead on the rooftop, another wounded. One of the stray rounds had severed an electrical wire in the roof, but the wisp of smoke went unnoticed as the helicopter descended to the roof to pick up the dead and wounded men. The rotor fanned the fire and, as the 'copter raised from the roof, the fire was visible.

The fire trucks simply could not get through the traffic, so they watched helplessly as the sky reddened. The fire eventually dispersed the looters, but by the time the first engine company managed to reach the scene, the building was fully engulfed in flames. What food remained inside was destroyed. By dawn, only the cement-block walls remained. Eleven people had died in the building, trapped by the fire. The Chicago incident was history. The amount of food stolen or salvaged was insignificant compared to that lost in the fire; it was estimated that the loss could have fed two thousand families for one year.

The Seattle incident was a direct result of the events in Chicago, well publicized by the news media. Much was made of the massive traffic jam and the inability of the police and fire personnel to reach the scene. Chicago was spontaneous; Seattle was planned, and planned well.

Frost Foods was, as in the Chicago incident, a food-chain warehouse located in a suburb of Seattle, the contents consisting totally of prepared frozen foods. On the evening of the incident, the weather was cold, with fog and a damp mist falling. No one noticed a lone individual cutting the power lines, followed by a large semitrailer truck backing up to the loading platform. About a dozen men exited from the rear of the trailer and, within seconds, the warehouse overhead door was open. The truck entered and the door closed behind it. During the night, twelve runs were made between the warehouse and a farm located about ten miles distant. At the farm, an orderly procession of cars moved in to collect the contraband delivered by the trucks. By dawn, both the farm and the warehouse were virtually empty. More than two thousand individuals had been involved in what was probably the largest planned mass robbery on record. Everything, including the trucks, had been stolen. The whole operation had been organized by twelve individuals meeting together but always wearing masks. The identities of those involved would never be known.

Seattle police pleaded with the media not to publicize the details, but to no avail. By the next day, the seeds were planted. Many asked the question, "If they can get away with it, why can't I?" The answer was to come in the forthcoming months as "food robs," as they became known, eventually became so common that the news media took no notice whatsoever.

The major cities were the first to succumb to the panic, and Washington, D.C., did not escape. It seemed that Congress and emergency legislation could not keep up with the crises. A number of congressmen, including Bumper Johnson, finally were able to convince the President to call a state of emergency. The country was placed under martial law by executive order. The armed forces, including the National Guard units, were mobilized to maintain order and to stop the "food robs." For a time the maneuver met with success; then the order began to break down, this time with the assistance of the troops. Some were corrupted by money, some did it for friends and families. Short of mass court martials, there was no stopping this attack.

Bumper was amazed at how quickly the country had been reduced to disorder. It was unsafe to carry any food on the streets of D.C. for fear of being robbed. One had to lock and guard whatever food one had in storage. Indeed, most of the restaurants had closed out of fear of being robbed. Bumper noticed that for the first time in many years, he was losing weight.

Using the spring elections as an excuse, but actually worried about their immediate families, Congress adjourned in mid-March.

Bumper once again headed for the farm. The trip this time was extremely difficult, with few gasoline stations open and no restaurants serving food of any kind. At one service station he noticed that the vending machine had been smashed and the food stolen. Everyone was armed. Bumper felt the fear of the front lines during World War II, only this time it was a war of shortage. Food was far more valuable than bullets.

The old farm never looked a more welcome sight, though a locked gate had been added, and John was armed with a rifle.

"Things that bad?" Bumper said, pointing at the weapon.

"I'm afraid so; we've had a few visitors around the place," John replied. "You look beat; come on in."

Bumper settled himself in the chair by the stove; he was asleep before Sherri could greet him. She had also wanted to be the first to tell him that she and John had been married last week.

"So you two tied the knot, eh? Didn't even bother to let me in on it." Bumper felt better later with the warm kitchen stove nearby and a breakfast of pancakes, bacon, and coffee.

"We're sorry, Senator. We just wanted to get married so we would have some time together before…" Sherri didn't finish, but they all knew what she was thinking.

"How long can you last up here?" Bumper asked.

John stared into his coffee cup as he answered, "Maybe a year if we're careful and things don't get much worse. We've got plenty of firewood, but if summer is late, our food won't last another winter. Mom closed the store this week; she can't stock the shelves and she's afraid of looters. I'm moving her out here tomorrow."

Strange, Bumper thought, *the old farm is to be their fortress against the ice and cold.* For the first time he began to wonder about chances of survival. How long, really, could they last? The snow fell quietly, covering his car and the road, and with it disappeared any chance of returning to D.C. in the foreseeable future. He turned to John.

"I'll help you get some more wood in for the stove."

For Dr. Olsson, D.C. was a living nightmare. Martial law had all but broken down completely nationally, and he didn't know how much longer the Houston base would stay together.

Warren's wife Sally had quietly organized an active opposition group, first at the base and now joined by hundreds of Houston natives. He knew that they had taken part in a number of food robs and were using part of the base as a supply cache. The only data collected from Solar III was through Charlie Richardson's personal efforts to maintain the monitors in some semblance of operation. Last week he told Gus Olsson that he did not know how much longer he could continue. The only food now available was controlled by various groups such as the one initiated by Sally and it was either join or starve. Even the President had retreated to his California vacation "White House" amid rumors that several cargo planes laden with food preceded him.

There seemed little reason to stay around and watch D.C. die as a city. Much of the food had already been looted from the stores, and he was certain that some people were slowly starving to death. The newspapers had ceased publication, and the only communication was via an occasional TV newscast. Time was running out. Within three days Gus had made his decision; he would attempt to fly to Houston and take his chances with Charlie. The marble city was fast becoming a cemetery.

Gus Olsson called Charlie and told him of his plans. He was quite certain that he would have to fly by himself because all D.C. bases were closed. Solar III had brought a kind of peace to the world—no one country could muster enough energy to wage war on another. Military planes required fuel, and that fuel was being used to keep people from freezing to death.

Dr. Olsson had maintained his combat pilot status; it was almost a pleasure to lift off into the cold sky. The fighter jet headed for Houston. He could land at the base and somehow make contact with Charlie. D.C. looked dead behind him. Almost no lights were visible on the ground. Gus wondered at the transformation of the country within a few months from the greatest power in the world to a shambles. Food was the common denominator; nothing else mattered. A once proud military force sent to guard the nation's food stores had become far worse than the element it was sent to resist. Unless a miracle occurred reversing the hellish cold, the nine-month survival prediction was, if anything, optimistic. Nine months to live; Gus passed away the flight time deciding what he'd best like to do during the time remaining. Flying to Houston was not high on his list of priorities. Nor was there much fun one could have, considering the general condition of the country.

He tried to contact Houston tower; there was no answer. Gus made for the base air strip. He had been there many times but, without lights, the landing was a decidedly tricky maneuver. He brought the fighter up to the deserted operations building and noticed a lone car, its lights on, off, on, off, twice. It was Charlie.

"Charlie, I'm sure glad to see you," Gus greeted him warmly. "Houston—is it as bad as D.C.?"

Charlie nodded. "Get in, I'll fill you in on the way."

They drove cautiously through the darkened streets.

"Things weren't too bad here till that Florida conference; why the hell did they have to televise that? Anyway, we had a rash of robberies until the troops moved in—that stopped it for a spell. Then, Christ, you wouldn't believe it. *They* started swiping everything in sight. We had one real bad shootout—killed about a hundred, and now you don't see a soul. They're all staying inside, keeping warm and saving their energy. The food's all been picked up; I've got some locked up at the base or I'd have nothing myself. I've been staying at base operations. They looted my apartment last week. Christ, Gus, we're at war with ourselves!"

They ate in the officers' kitchen. Charlie grilled some hamburgers and heated the three-day-old coffee.

"Sorry, I can't do any better," he apologized.

"Fine by me," Gus thanked him. "Say, where did everybody go?"

Charlie sipped the hot, rank brew.

"The ones with families left as soon as the looting started. They didn't want to be away from home, so I let them off. I couldn't keep any of the others after that; other than a few officers living at the Bachelor Officers Quarters, I'm alone. I've tried to keep the monitor on Solar III operational, but that's about it."

Gus interrupted him. "I'd like to see it if it's running."

"Sure Gus, Let's go on over now; I never know if the damn thing is operational until I switch the power on."

They made their way through the darkened hallways, their footsteps echoing in the emptiness of the place. Charlie switched the lights and power on.

"We still have power out here—at least as long as I have fuel for the generators."

Gus watched the screen. "So this is where it all started." He spoke almost reverently, in a whisper. Charlie nodded. and they both sat silently watching the data display. The trend was still downward.

"I can't tell if there has been any change," Charlie commented. "The computer has been down for the last month."

Bathed in the ghostly green light of the display, neither man noticed two figures appear in the doorway to the monitor room.

The woman spoke first: "Freeze!"

Gus and Charlie raised their hands slowly and turned to face a man and a woman both armed with rifles.

"Christ!" Charlie muttered under his breath. "It's Sally!"

She evidently heard him. "Right you are. Now all we want is the food."

"How did you get in?" Charlie asked, incredulous.

She glared at him. "That son-of-a-bitch left his pass keys when he took off with that whore, Lynn What's-her-name. Now you just show us the food."

Her partner was silent; he was a stranger to Charlie. Gus motioned to Charlie.

"Come on, we'd better go along with them."

The four walked slowly down the aisle toward the commissary, Charlie desperately trying to think of a trap. The food was stored in a locker located in the basement of the assembly building. They would have to walk along the corridor between the units, down the stairs, and through another corridor to the cold storage locker. Dividing the buildings were large fire doors hidden in the walls and powered by air pistons. They were designed to close in the event of a fire alarm. Charlie figured that if he could get enough distance between them, closing the door would isolate them from the fugitives. The doors could be hand released by breaking the glass on a wall-mounted fire pull box.

Charlie moved over towards Gus and whispered, "Walk faster, I've a plan."

Sally saw their exchange. "Any more talk and you get a bullet in the back."

Charlie decided to wait until they reached the lower corridor before making the attempt. Descending the stairs would allow him an excuse to move toward the wall. He would need at least ten feet to allow the fire door to close between them.

Sally did not seem to notice their quickened pace. As Charlie and Gus passed by the door, Charlie hit the fire box with a quick jab of his elbow and at the same time yelled at Gus, "Hit the deck!"

The door shot across the hallway as Sally pumped a fusillade of bullets into the steel plate that separated them.

"Okay, Gus, let's get out of here fast."

Charlie waited long enough for Gus to get to his feet, and the two of them raced down the hall.

"Here," Charlie pointed, "we'll take the elevator up the quartermaster supplies—there're some rifles in there."

Arming themselves, they returned to the main level.

"We've got to find them now," Gus whispered. "They know that the food is stored on the lower level, and I bet they're trying to break into the locker. Warren's key wouldn't fit that lock."

"Okay," Charlie answered. "Let's head back down there."

The two men made their way carefully back to the locker area; at the end of the hall they noticed that the frozen food storage area door was open.

"They must have shot the lock off," Charlie commented.

Moving quietly down the hall, guns ready, they approached the locker.

As he stood beside the door, Charlie yelled, "Come out with your hands up."

The response was a round of gunfire from within the room. Charlie had had enough; he jumped into the room emptying a clip of ammunition as he did so. There was no response. Gus cautiously entered. Charlie was standing over two forms on the floor; Sally and her companion were dead. It was six months to the day of the launch date of Solar III.

13. Sinking

Iceland had fared better than much of the world during the freeze. The combination of a small population and enough good equipment to withstand the winter was an asset in this war. The government had imposed strict controls on visitors, not allowing anyone new on the island. There had been some looting in Reykjavik, but as far as Warren and Lynn were concerned, their life had been unaffected until this last month. Work had been progressing on the project, and food was no more limited than usual during the Icelandic winter.

The first hint of trouble came via a meeting called by the project manager. He had asked for an extension of the deep water pier, presumably to make ready for some unknown freighter. The change seemed odd because the turbines were not to be delivered until next summer. Then why the dock?

The addition to the dock had taken just under two months to complete. Within a week, a freighter of questionable origin appeared in the fjord. After considerable difficulty, the ship was positioned broadside to the recently completed dock. Whatever her reason for being in Stongsfjörd, one thing was certain: she was empty. Her waterline was high, showing a good seven feet of rusting bottom.

She was manned by a crew of shabbily dressed seamen who for the most part stayed with the ship. For the better part of a week, there was no activity, and then, late Friday evening, she started taking on cargo: food, their food for the project.

By Saturday morning, word had spread around the entire group: food was being transferred somewhere, and every case placed aboard that ship lessened their chances of survival at Stongsfjörd. The rumor had it that a luxury resort was being stocked for an elite clientele of wealthy patrons, where food stores were to be adequate for several years. The rumor was in fact true. Guam had been picked as a retreat for five hundred of the world's richest families, one of them the owner of the Stongsfjörd Construction Company. The ship was to be loaded and ready to sail in one week.

Saturday at noon, a small group of men met at Warren and Lynn's living unit. They were there for one purpose: to plan how to stop the food from leaving Stongsfjörd. The first order was to disable the ship, and second, to secure the food stores against whoever was trying to steal them. The ship had to be scuttled before any more food was transferred on board. Saturday night had to be the time.

The plan agreed upon was quite simple, if it worked. One of the crew would be mugged and replaced by a worker at Stongsfjörd. A food box would be repacked with dynamite and a timed fuse, carried on board by the worker disguised in the crew member's clothes. The explosive would be placed against the hull below the water line.

They hoped the ship did not have automatic bulkhead doors. If not—enough compartments could flood to sink her. Warren was chosen to place the charge, and three men from the blast house would procure the dynamite in their lunch boxes.

"One thing bothers me about this," Lynn spoke up. "Who runs this place anyway, and what will they do when we try to sink their ship?"

It was a good question. The only manager other than the foreman was Ray Mosby, a quiet individual who kept to himself and limited his active participation in the project to staff meetings. There was an office in Reykjavik, but no one at the site had ever been there, with the possible exception of Mosby.

"The only guy who might have set us up, or knows about that damn ship, is Mosby. He could radio for help fast. We've got to shut him up before we try anything."

The man speaking was John O'Connor, a strong, heavyset individual, well versed in the ways of conflict. He was one of Warren's best men.

"Let's take Mosby right after dinner tonight before we hit the ship," John continued. "He also has some rifles in that gun cabinet in his office—they might just come in handy."

Before the group disbanded for the afternoon, a plan had been completed acceptable to all present. During dinner, John O'Connor would enter Mosby's office and lock him in the security vault. He would then return with the firearms to Warren and Lynn's to await the others. The dynamite would be placed in a champagne case and hand-carried by Warren "for the captain's table." Once on board, he could make his way below. When the ship blew, they would have to hope that no messages for assistance would be sent.

By plan, John O'Connor was absent from the dinner that evening. Warren told those who noticed that he wasn't feeling well.

Outside Mosby's office, John waited for some sign of activity inside. He'd never been in the building and so he would have to rely on his observations for direction. A light in a rear room revealed Mosby's outline at a desk containing a small radio transmitter-receiver. This evidently was the communication link with the head office.

John made his way quietly to the front of the building and tried the door; it was open. He made certain that no one was watching, then entered. The room evidently was a combination office and living quarters. In the dim light, John could make out a bed and cookstove, along with a large desk covered with papers and drawings. He positioned himself by the door to Mosby's radio room and listened.

"The bastards will be up when they find out about the food stores." It was Mosby speaking to an unknown receiver. "Yeah, I know, but I've got to wait until the stuff is loaded till I can get out. No, none that I know, all the guns are here in the office. I'll have everything out by tomorrow night. I expect to be taken care of for this."

John tightened his grip on a short length of iron pipe that he'd brought alone; Mosby had to come out of that room sooner or later.

He waited about an hour before Mosby got up, closed the desk, and opened the door. John came down hard with the pipe. The blow struck Mosby on the back of his head. Mosby crumpled, silent.

Using the light from the rear office, John dragged Mosby into the wall safe and propped him against a shelf. He closed and locked the inner gate, but left the massive outer door open. Mosby wouldn't suffocate, but the gate would hold him.

There were six automatic rifles and two pistols in the gun cabinet along with several boxes of ammunition. *Dammit,* he'd have to make two trips to get it all out. John grabbed the rifles and tucked the pistols in his jacket. He switched the light out in the rear office and made his way back to Warren and Lynn's unit. The dinner hour eliminated any concern about being seen. Still, he was cautious and breathed a sign of relief when the first batch of guns had been hidden.

His second trip went more slowly. The ammunition was heavy and, though John was a man of unusual strength, he had to rest on his return. After leaving the supplies at Warren and Lynn's, he went back to his own room and crawled into bed. Strain had exhausted him. His portion of the mission had been accomplished. The one thing John O'Connor didn't know was that Ray Mosby was dead. The blow had been fatal.

The group in Warren and Lynn's unit were busy far into the night. The dynamite had to be packed into the champagne crate and the timer rigged to the blasting cap. The rifles and ammunition were divided among the group. Around 11:00 P.M., a lone figure emerged from the living unit carrying a wooden crate. Warren's night had begun.

He walked slowly toward the dock, where he observed a cargo hoist still loading supplies. Whatever was on board now would be lost. A steep gangplank led to one of the lower decks; no one was visible. Warren quickly reached the deck and entered a gangway marked "forward hold." His task was incredibly easy. There was no evidence of any crew, and within five minutes he had placed the case of dynamite between the hull and one of the deck support beams. He estimated that the spot was six to eight feet below the water line.

Success made Warren careless. On his way topside, he made a wrong turn and shortly heard the words, "Halt, or I'll shoot!"

Warren turned to face an officer, pistol in hand.

"What are you doing on board?" the officer demanded.

"Nothing," Warren replied. "Just looking around." He glanced at his watch and noted the time. The dynamite was set to go off in approximately ten minutes. "I'm from Texas in America; guess I've never seen such a big ship," Warren lied. The officer was obviously American too.

"Texas eh? Well, the captain said to keep everybody off, and I guess that includes Texans." He motioned with his pistol—"The captain might like to talk to you; he don't like strangers on board."

Warren walked slowly, faking a limp. He had to kill a few minutes more.

"Come on, hurry it up there." The officer was impatient, but Warren managed a stiff leg climb for the stairways and hoped the timer was accurate.

The blast occurred as the two of them made their way along the main deck—Warren was amazed at the force. The ship gave a violent jerk, sending both Warren and the officer to the deck. Warren was up first, heading for the gangplank. The officer grabbed his pistol and followed.

The first shot was so close to Warren's ear he could hear the bullet buzz by. He made a frantic jump for the gangplank, missed, and splashed into the icy harbor. The chill numbed him for an instant, then he grabbed the base of a piling and pulled himself out of the water. Climbing onto the dock, he ran as fast as he could to the safety of the warehouse.

It had been a close call, but all the attention was on the ship, already listing slightly away from the dock. Warren watched hypnotized. Within ten minutes the ship was on her side, another ten and she rolled. Five members of the crew jumped and survived, but Warren's officer was not among them.

Freezing, Warren made his way back. Lynn took one look at him, then shoved Warren, clothes and all, into a hot shower.

"Hon, I damn near didn't make it," he told her. Then the cold and shock hit him and he could hardly talk.

Later, as they lay in bed together, he tried to tell her what had happened, but Lynn put her hand over his mouth, then pulled him to her. An hour earlier Warren had been certain that his days were over for everything, much less for love. Lynn really sustained him physically and mentally; sinking ships was not his fortune at all.

Before the wakeup call woke Warren and Lynn, the others had been busy. Ray Mosby had been found and given a simple burial, and the crew's five survivors had been transported to Reykjavik. Of the ship, part of the keel and rudder were all that was visible above water. For his first sinking, Warren had done an admirable job. The sound of the breakfast bell reminded the couple that they had overslept.

The meeting after breakfast was attended by all; the overturned hull in the harbor gave rise to plenty of curiosity. John O'Connor was the spokesman. He had the qualities of a natural leader. The attempt to remove the food, Mosby's death, and the banishment of the crew were mentioned briefly, along with a proposal for the future. The group would elect officers and organize for survival. A security force would be recruited and work efforts would be directed toward construction of steam-heated greenhouses to supplement the food supply. Those who wished to leave would be given transportation to Reykjavik; those staying would have to abide by the wishes of the majority. Only a handful chose to leave.

The group that had plotted the takeover met that evening to plan the governmental body, hold the elections, and draw up a simple constitution.

Within a day, the elections were held with John O'Connor being elected chairman, and Warren, along with two others, directors. A guard roster was made up, and Lynn was placed in charge of the food service. A commissary was to be opened so that each individual or family could draw their daily share of the rations and use only as much as they wished. Food allocations were planned for two years; after that one could only guess.

The evening came, clear and cold, and with it a return to normal at Stongsfjörd. Except for the dead and the ship lying upside down on the bottom of the harbor, it had been an ordinary weekend. The need for food had changed a team of willing workers to an army, dug in against the hellish weather, with but one common thought—survival.

14.
Evacuation

No single element of the world's population had fared any worse than the large city dweller. His life was totally dependent on others to supply his needs. As their sources were depleted, those who had survived became nomads, wandering about the countryside, seeking food and shelter. Those who attempted to rob others were often shot; others died from exposure to the cold. Stores, offices, high-rise apartments—all were deserted, and with the desertion came fire, fires that burned for days, uncontrolled, leaving burned-out skeletons where once modern structures stood filled with people, animals, and provisions.

At first, attempts were made to control the holocausts. A few firefighters remained loyal to their duties and fought the flames. Aircraft loaded with water "bombs" were used, but the fires had become uncontrollable. The burning continued generally until a natural barrier was reached such as a river or lake. Only then did the fires subside, leaving desolation in their wake.

At first the television networks carried the news of the fires. Then, as the studios themselves were consumed in the flames, coverage stopped. World communications gradually ceased, and except for some government and military channels, the countries of the world were left in isolation. For the group at Stongsfjörd, news of friends and relatives and their plight was impossible to obtain. Warren at times thought of Sally. His concern gradually changed to curiosity. Then, with the news blackout, their isolation made the U.S. seem years distant. Time at Stongsfjörd was measured in units of food rations and how fast the solar greenhouses could be completed for the production of fresh produce.

After the shooting incident, Charlie Richardson and Gus Olsson made a valiant effort to get information from Solar III and relay it to D.C. They secured the operations building against looters and food robs, and they maintained contact with the satellite for about two weeks.

Their work was interrupted once by a garbled message from D.C.: "City is evacuating, return at once, we cannot make further contact, repeat, return."

Gus picked up the message and turned to Charlie.

"We've had it now, my boy."

They stared out the window at the frozen landscape, white snow covering the frozen palm trees.

"Gus, how do we get back?" Charlie had a good point.

"Charlie, I think we'd better load up as much of that food as we can into one of the twins, and hope like hell we can find enough fuel to get back."

The two men spent the next three days loading food into an old twin-engine turboprop training plane. The aircraft was obsolete, but rugged, and could carry a substantial payload. To get the necessary fuel, they siphoned several of the other aircraft wing tanks that were still full, awaiting a mission never to be called. The end of the week saw them ready to head north to D.C.

Charlie had gathered all of the Solar III data. With reluctance, he cut the generator power to the monitor. Houston base was officially dead. A stop at a simple grave in the administrative building courtyard was the last duty of the two men; Sally and her unknown companion were laid to rest there. They turned to go. It was strangely silent around the base now. Nothing really mattered except to reach D.C. and report in.

The plane droned down the runway and was off. In the frost of the morning, a cold wind rattled the hangar door, left ajar in their hasty departure.

It was a strange sensation for the two men, both accomplished pilots, to fly without any radio contact. All of the major airports were closed, and except for a few military aircraft, nothing was in the air. Below on the ground, a number of fires flickered, out of control and left to burn. The pits of hell could look no more terrifying or desolate.

The approach to D.C. National Airport was no less a shock than their departure: no tower contact and no runway lights. They made two passes with the landing lights on to make certain the runway was clear and then let down. They taxied to the base courtesy hanger and left the plane and cargo inside. No one would look inside the aircraft for food, they hoped. There was no waiting limousine, but a search of the motor pool resulted in a jeep, its gas tank half full, evidently in running condition.

The ride to quarters was a cold experience in the open vehicle, but better than on foot. Arriving at the quarters, the two men split up, thankful that there was still power and heat in the buildings.

"I'll call you tomorrow," Gus called as they parted.

"Okay." Then Charlie was gone.

Gus spent a good half hour languishing in a hot tub and then, his body relaxed after the strain of the flight, he went directly to bed.

The dining hall, usually filled with several hundred men for breakfast, was empty except for a dozen or so individuals serving themselves coffee and cold cereal. Gus met Charlie at the coffee service.

"God, where have they gone?" Charlie questioned, pointing to the empty room.

"I don't know. I couldn't get anything up at the office either, though the orderly is supposed to be in at six."

Gus had tried to phone various people several times without an answer. He was anxious to get over to the office.

They parked the jeep in the office building's underground lot, also vacant, and took the elevator to the office. Gus noticed that there were no security guards. The empty halls echoed to their feet; the building was deserted. His desk, piled high with mail, had not been touched in several days. Dust had settled on the glass top. A note from his secretary Mary was taped to the back of his chair. It told a brief story.

"Listen to this, Charlie." Gus read the contents. "We were all released Thursday, no food, and the stores are all closed. We have to take care of our families now. Good-bye and good luck, Dr. Olsson."

The two men stared at each other for a few moments, and then Charlie spoke. "One hell of a way to lose an army, I'd say."

Gus laughed then became serious. "For our own welfare, we'd better get that food out of the plane and to the quarters." He grabbed two parkas from his closet. "Let's go."

At the hangar, the two men located a covered trailer and loaded the supplies. The effort took most of the morning, and by noon, they had left the field once again for quarters. Then they unloaded their cargo into one of the commissary food-storage lockers, long since emptied of its contents when, in their departure, the base personnel had helped themselves. Gus pulled a heavy brass padlock from his pocket.

"This is the best I could find—it might slow someone down a little."

They took enough canned stew for supper, locked the door and headed for the dining area. Tonight Charlie and Gus were all alone. They warmed the stew and reheated the coffee. A meager meal, but more than millions around the earth were enjoying.

After dinner the two men returned to Charlie's room armed with a coffeepot and a loaf of bread. They sat silent for a spell, looking out at a dull red glow on the horizon. The fires were starting in D.C.

"It's south of here, I think," Gus spoke softly, "moving up the other side of the Potomac."

Charlie glanced at a photo on the wall of an Air Force fighter bomber.

"Christ, what a chance for them to attack us." Gus laughed. "Y'know, that's what's so damn funny about this—the world's at peace because all the armies are starving."

It was true; no one country could wage war on another without food—the ultimate price for world peace was world starvation.

They watched the glow in silence for almost two hours. It would flare up for a few moments and then die down. Thousands were probably fleeing in front of the red wall, taking nothing but their lives with them. Somehow an army is accustomed to war and death. It's their profession. But this fire was something different. For those involved, there was no fighting back—only running.

"Gus, I think I'll turn in." Charlie spoke in the darkness. "If that fire jumps the river, we'll be out of here to heaven knows where tomorrow."

Charlie stared at the scene outside the window. "Good night, Gus." *God, he thought, almost in prayer, what have we done to deserve this?*

It was not the strange red glow of the fire that awoke Gus about dawn; it was the sound, a sound as if someone were moaning from pain, in the distance. He listened for a few moments before rising and going over to the window. Silhouetted against the crimson sky were thousands of people, moving as a wave before the flames. They had crossed the bridge to avoid a fiery death, and now were headed up the boulevard towards the base. Gus jumped into his clothes and ran down the hall to wake Charlie.

"Charlie, it must be half the city! Get up, man, and look."

Charlie peered out the window at the sight. He wished he'd stayed in Houston.

"Come on, Charlie, get dressed. We've got to do something before they mob the place. See if you can reach headquarters on the phone."

Pulling on his trousers, Charlie picked up the phone and listened for a moment.

"It's dead, Gus. Fire must have cut the lines."

"Damn," Gus cursed. "We'd better get out to the main gate and see if we can organize that mob."

The two men ran down the stairs and made for the main gate on the run, Gus stopping for a moment in the guard house to grab a bullhorn. By the time they reached the gate, the first people had arrived. They were strangely quiet, covered with the soot and ashes of the fire; many had only nightclothes on under a bathrobe or jacket. The cold caused them to huddle as others joined the group. The scene reminded Gus of prison camp liberation after World War II, yet now he looked upon people who only a few months ago had enjoyed the riches of one of the world's most affluent cities. Now they were refugees fleeing an inferno.

Gus got on the bullhorn.

"Line up at the gate. We will lead you to shelter."

He kept repeating the message, and slowly an endless line began to form.

Turning to Charlie, he said, "Get them over to the assembly building and see if you can recruit some volunteers to go over to medical supply for first aid gear. A lot of them have burns."

Charlie nodded, and Gus opened the gate to the line. They came in almost cautiously, many in a state of shock. How many, one could only guess; there must have been several thousand.

Up ahead Charlie got them started into the assembly building, out of the cold, and then picked a dozen of the most able-bodied men to haul the first aid supplies. An hour passed, and they were still coming through the gate; Gus left it open and made his way along the lines to the assembly building.

Gus and Charlie worked all day and into the night organizing teams for first aid, food preparation, and lodging. The base, which had a capacity for thirty thousand troops, would be filled to capacity by evening. The food would not last long and the heating and lighting would last only as long as there was fuel for the boilers. For as long as things held out, the refugee camp would save them. People such as these counted minutes.

Exhausted, Charlie and Gus gave up around midnight and walked slowly back to their quarters, now crowded with people. Several watched through the window at the end of the hall as the fire spread to the city center. The "firewind" sped the flames on their destructive path; by morning there would be only darkened marble skeletons. The capitol dome collapsed at 12:53 A.M. Gus and Charlie turned in shortly after 1:00 A.M.

The next morning, the assembly building served breakfast to more people than at any time since World War II. Thousands at least got coffee, milk, and toast, with a few of the more fortunate receiving eggs or bacon. This group was the only major surviving element in D.C. For tens of thousands who were trapped in the false security of the subways, the heat and smoke were fatal. The group at the base sensed the horror, and none wished to return. For the moment, the base, spared by the river and the wind, was home for them.

Charlie and Gus sat at a corner table watching the sea of humanity before them. Both men were career officers with families, yet the sight was far worse than any war memory. Having refugees in your own country was a different matter, refugees from the war of the elements.

Charlie looked at Gus and, half in jest, said, "Now what?"

"I don't know, Charlie. We have no command here anymore, that's for certain. Unless you have a better idea, it's back to Houston."

Charlie was silent for a moment, then he replied, "Yes, we still have a chance—if we can get enough fuel in that old crate to get back, there's still a hell of a lot of food in that locker. We sure blew our supply here on this crew."

Gus smiled, "I guess so, but I must be getting old. I'm tired of running from this thing, but just too stubborn to call it quits, I guess."

The jeep started easily, and the two soldiers turned the base over to what was left of D.C. The food might last two to three weeks, Gus thought, but they had done all that they could. A few might survive, somehow.

The task of obtaining fuel from the other aircraft consumed most of their afternoon, but by dusk Gus and Charlie had enough to make Houston. A few of the refugees watched their takeoff, but otherwise the departure went unnoticed. They made a brief pass over the city. Below lay almost total destruction. Once proud buildings were starkly outlined in black where walls were left standing, funeral colors.

"Head her south, Gus. I don't want to see any more of it."

"Yeah, I understand," commented Gus, as the plane turned toward Houston. "If only you could fight this damn thing, you'd feel a little better."

The engines droned on through the night.

Houston base was unchanged. Vandals and fire had as yet spared this city. After securing the aircraft, Charlie and Gus dined on their first meal since that early breakfast, how long before? There was quite a store of food in the lockers, and initially they both thought of staying there. Then Charlie raised the question of security. How could the two of them secure the place? There were surely others like Sally, and sooner or later their luck would run out.

Charlie suddenly remembered Sand Cay, a practice strip out in the Gulf of Mexico about seventy miles off the coast. Once a resort, the island had been taken over during World War II as a submarine patrol lookout, and more recently used for radar missions. The old homestead stood at one end with a lighthouse, and a radar tower was at the other end. A landing strip and two weather-beaten hangars completed the improvements.

"Gus, there's a small island out in the Gulf that we used to use for practice landings. I don't know what's left of the place, but it would be easy to secure. Why don't we load up the plane with what food is left around here and get the hell out?"

Gus thought for a moment. Charlie was right; they would not have much of a chance protecting the Houston base. They could try to make radio contact with others, but for that matter they didn't even know where the President was. A few days before the fire, a rumor had circulated to the effect that the presidential party had flown to Hawaii. Islands were becoming popular retreats.

"I guess it's as good a place as any, Charlie. You sure we can land out there? Fuel is getting short."

Gus remembered that they had drained the tanks of the other aircraft to reach D.C. How much additional fuel was left was questionable.

"They used to bring some big stuff in out there," Charlie replied. "I'm sure the strip is still there."

"Okay," said Gus, "we can load up tomorrow morning."

Midmorning the next day saw a lone plane headed out over the Gulf of Mexico. Smoke was rising from an oil refinery fire; the burning of Houston had begun.

They made two low passes over Sand Cay before landing in order to survey the island. From the air it appeared deserted but intact. The old plane came in for its final landing, bumped along the strip, and taxied up to a small administration building and tower. Windows were broken, and the door banged open against the wall in the wind. There was no other sound.

"Well, Gus, let's have a look around," suggested Charlie as he opened the cabin door.

"This would be a nice place if it weren't so damn cold," commented Gus as he pulled his parka hood over his head. The temperature was below freezing, and the wind blew hard.

They walked to the old homestead standing alone on the only high ground on the Cay. Years ago the building had been a retreat for an exclusive Houston fishing club; then with the coming of World War II that ended. Acquired by the government, the homestead had served its last years as a barracks, mess hall, operations center, and radar room. Other than a few broken windows, the place looked usable.

"We're in luck, Gus. The radio equipment is still here." Charlie made a quick survey of the equipment. With a little luck they could get it operational. They could then try to contact others to determine the state of the world.

Using an old wagon, they gradually moved the food supplies to the homestead and dismantled the radio equipment from the aircraft. They would try to use it at the homestead. They also patched the broken windows and got the old space heater functioning. There was a small emergency generator set, and they decided to use it for the radios only and rely on kerosene lanterns for lighting. The cook stove was also kerosene, giving rise to the guess that there were underground storage tanks on the Cay. They would spend tomorrow looking around the remainder of the island.

They ate well that evening. The two men, tired of running, were grateful to be able to relax and enjoy a complete and quiet meal. Outside, the wind blew cold and dead leaves rattled on the palms. At one time the Cay had been pretty, with well manicured lawns and the tall stately palms. Now all was brown, dead; no coconuts would ever again grow from the palms. Yet the homestead was warm, and the flickering glow of the kerosene lamps was pleasant.

After dinner, the two men sat in silence watching the amber glow in the sky to the north.

"Must be one hell of a fire," Gus said.

"Yeah, I think Houston's really getting it now," answered Charlie.

Indeed, the city was "getting it." Fires were spreading from the refineries north along the canal. Ahead of the flames, as in D.C., the people fled. Behind them lay flaming embers and the dead.

Exhausted, the two men pulled two bunks into the main room and turning down the stove, climbed into sleeping bags, and fell asleep. Outside, a light snow fell, covering the ground, the first snow in the island's recorded history. Snow was also falling in Houston, but no one noticed.

Sand Cay was quiet the next day save for the voices of the two men and a few birds. Three inches of new snow covered the ground, and the men were glad that they had made the flight the day before. They would not have been able to see the runway today. They located the fuel storage area and, to their surprise, several of the tanks were full of kerosene; fuel would not be a problem in the near future. The lighthouse was not functioning, but nevertheless it would provide a good lookout tower.

A small garage housed an old army truck that would probably run with a little attention; the tools would also come in handy.

The operations building was a shambles. Vandals had broken most of the windows, and the weather had completed the job. The building was adjacent to one beach, and this had led to its demise.

Most of the other buildings, hidden in the scrub, had escaped; vandals are a lazy lot.

Charlie worked on the radio most of the afternoon; he used the old wireless antenna and recharged the batteries using the small diesel generator set. In spite of being old, the equipment was rugged and usable. Toward nightfall, he started searching the band for stations. Static was all the reward he received for his efforts.

"Wait till after dark, Charlie," Gus commented. "Look what I found on the beach."

Gus held up a full bottle of Scotch whiskey, evidently left by a picnicking party in happier days. Now it was a rare treat, and the two men sat by the stove enjoying the luxury. They agreed to have only one drink every week—this would extend their newly found pleasure. Outside the wind was picking up. The true first winter storm was upon them.

After dinner the two men watched and listened to the storm grow in intensity. The surf was pounding on the beach, pushed by the howling wind. Unknown to Gus and Charlie, a flotilla of yachts attempting to escape the fires in Houston had been lost in the storm. Their superstructures coated with ice caused the boats to capsize. Inland, the wind fanned the flames into a frenzy. City blocks were engulfed in a matter of minutes. All went unnoticed by the two men on the island, isolated by the storm.

For Senator Johnson, the isolation was extremely difficult. He was an individual used to being with people and the activity that went along with a senator's life. Their radio had carried the news of the burning of D.C. Bumper could not yet accept the fact that his way of life and the city had both been destroyed. Each day, he walked into town from the farm to the meeting house. At least there was a chance of conversation and the exchange of rumors. What bothered him most was the complete lack of concern people showed for the end of the government as they had known it. Life seemed to go on, and except for the absence of much activity, the town showed little outward change. The city ski crowd usually accounted for most of the winter business and traffic, but this year there were no skiers. Bumper tried to answer questions as best he could. All were concerned about the growing season, for without it, they could not replenish their food stores.

The date when the geese usually arrived came and passed; snow still lay heavy on the fields and ice covered the millpond. Clouds often covered the sun now, adding to the chill. Even the children felt the cold and stayed indoors. The school was closed; wood to heat it could be put to better use.

They had enough food at the farm, but they were trying to conserve as much as possible. Fish from the millpond often substituted for meat. Ice fishing had become the town's main pastime.

Yet they were fortunate. Towns nearer the large cities had been ransacked by looters, with open warfare developing between the residents and the outsiders. Further north, the unplowed roads effectively blocked all traffic.

During the evenings, the four of them sat by the parlor stove and searched the radio band for a station still reporting. John had rigged an antenna in the attic to improve the reception so they would have contact as long as the batteries lasted in the radio.

It seemed from the reports that almost every major city was ablaze throughout the world, and following the fires, disease and starvation took their toll. There had been estimates that a third to half the world's population had perished, a number beyond belief. Several religious broadcasters were still active, preaching that the end of the earth had arrived. This was small comfort to those still alive and able to listen. *Perhaps,* Bumper thought, *this is preordained, and if so, how many will be allowed to survive? Better not to dwell on that thought.* He looked at John and Sherri, and prayed that they would be spared. So far, the town had been fortunate. Other than two people killed in a farmhouse fire, the population was the same as before the onset of Solar III.

15.
Slide

The Stongsfjörd community had turned to the tasks of building the greenhouses and rationing food. Some were dissatisfied, but for the most part life in the community was stable. To Warren and Lynn, life was almost pleasant except for the terrible haunting fear that food supplies would run out eventually.

Their immediate task had been to rebuild and equip a small building high on the ridge as a communications center. Originally constructed as a weather station, it had been abandoned with the development of the Stongsfjörd community. Radio equipment, a tall antenna, and living quarters had been installed in the building, along with food stores. A steam line from a thermal geyser on the other side of the ridge provided heat. A small generator set ran when the radio was operational.

The building was both a good security lookout and radio station. Couples would take turns manning the building when it was completed. Warren and Lynn enjoyed the work; they could be together, and the effort kept their minds from worries of the future. A large map of the world was mounted on a wall with coded flag pins to show locations of radio contacts around the world. Information could thus be gained as to the number of survivors, their location and condition. If there were any chance that some might live through the solar dimming, this information would provide a basis to begin again. They all needed that hope at Stongsfjörd.

Security was another matter. In the event someone sighted an approaching group, an alarm would be sounded and a select band of riflemen would be sent out to meet and determine the group's intent. It had been decided that any additions to the population at

Stongsfjörd would have to be approved by council vote, because the existing food supply would be affected.

"The outpost," as the building became known, was a popular addition. From the date of completion, there was no lack of volunteers for duty, and the map began to fill with small flags. White indicated a contact, and black was substituted when a station was lost. In addition, a logbook maintained a written record of population, names, and exact locations of contact stations. There was a constant exchange of questions concerning the condition of relatives and friends. There was always the hope that someone had survived.

Fire, followed by disease, had taken its toll. There was not a single radio contact within a major population center. The size of the surviving groups ranged from one individual to several thousand. Indeed, the world's "radio" population was estimated by the Stongsfjörd records to be less than two million. How many others had survived at this point would never be known.

During their second tour of duty at the outpost, Lynn was reading the log while Warren scanned the various frequencies for contacts. The procedure was first to reconfirm all of the existing stations before searching for any new ones. As each contact was made, Lynn entered the time and information in the log while checking the map flags. The operation took several hours to complete; then a break would be made for a meal and four hours of sleep, followed by the final search for new contacts.

Lynn had made her way through about half of the log when an entry made the day before stopped her cold. It read, "USA, Sand Cay, Texas, two men C.A. Richardson and G. Olsson, appear to be military survivors." An additional paragraph described the burning of Houston and notes on the weather.

"War! My God, look!" Lynn pushed the logbook in front of him.

"It can't be!" he said in amazement as he spun the dial to the correct frequency.

Lynn grabbed his hand. "What are you going to tell them, War? If we put this in the log, everyone here will blame us for this mess. War, we can't take the chance."

Warren paused for a moment. "Yeah, I guess so, but let's talk to them anyway—we won't use our names. Hell, they'll never make the connection."

Lynn was firm. "No names, War. I mean it." He knew she did.

Charlie came in clear. "Ice, this is Sand Cay." The Stongsfjörd call code name was "Ice"—quite fitting, Warren thought.

"Hear you clear, Sand Cay," Warren replied. "How are you?"

"Okay, Ice. We've got a storm now, about a foot of snow since dawn. Mainland bad, Houston burned, New Orleans burning, also Monterrey. How are you?"

"Good we didn't stay," whispered Lynn.

Warren turned to the mike. "Ice okay, no change, weather clear and cold, minus twenty-one degrees Fahrenheit now, not much snow. We are stable." Warren paused a moment, then, "Where is your home? Any survivors?"

Charlie came back on. "I'm from Houston, and Olsson is from Washington, D.C. Both cities burned. We don't know about any survivors."

Warren paused. Then, "Thanks, Sand Cay. Will call tomorrow. Good luck." He signed off.

Warren and Lynn sat speechless for a moment. It had to be Charlie and Gus; hell, it even sounded like Charlie. God, if they could only identify themselves without letting the others know. They could find out about everything that had happened since their departure. Dammit, there had to be a way.

They completed the remainder of the scan without much interest, recorded the contacts, and then shut down the generator for their meal. To avoid the individuals having to haul their own food, supplies had been brought up to the outpost during its reconstruction. Each couple was on the honor system to use only what food was necessary. Lynn made up some biscuits along with a can of vegetables and dried beef. They split a chocolate candy bar for dessert, along with some hot coffee. Afterward, they sat thinking again of the contact with Charlie and Gus and tried to figure out how to identify themselves. Finally Warren shrugged.

"I give up, hon. Let's go to bed and get our four hours." Lynn nodded, and they got into their sleeping bags for the night. Silence descended on the outpost.

The earth's crust is a fragile thing, floating on a fluid of liquid rock, constantly vying for position with the oceans. Few people, save the geologists who study such phenomena, understand the tremendous forces at odds, constantly shifting the continents inch by inch, year by year. When these forces exceed certain limits, earthquakes result. The earth's crust had withstood the cooling effect of the solar dimming for these months. Now it was to give way.

Warren woke up on the floor of the outpost. The entire building was shaking, and some of the radio gear had already crashed to the floor. Lynn was still in her lower bunk trying to get free of her sleeping bag. Warren dragged her to the door and outside into the cold. Lights were on in the compound and people were screaming. The ground moved in undulating waves, making it difficult to stand.

Then the roar started; first a rumble, then an ear-shattering roar, and within seconds, silence. The entire side of the mountain opposite them had given way. Stongsfjörd was buried under thousands of tons of rock rubble, entombed. The smell of rock dust permeated the night air. But now it was totally silent; the earthquake had lasted seven minutes. The fault underlying the settlement had shifted thirty inches, not a great distance, but for a mountain of rock—too much.

The couple turned to stare inside the outpost, peering through the dust. Warren located a flashlight. The beam of light exposed a shambles. Most of the radio equipment was on the floor mixed in with broken dishes and glassware.

"Oh God," Lynn sobbed. "Why doesn't this damn world just kill us and get it over with?"

Warren looked at her. She was terrified, her face almost as white as the snow.

"You stay here, hon. I'll get dressed and go down the hill." She sat down on the remains of the bunk and he covered her with a blanket. The cold draft told of the broken windows and heaven knows what else.

Since the path was strewn with rocks and rubble, he picked his way carefully to avoid injury. At the base of the slope, the path ended abruptly. A wall of rock, Warren could not tell how high or deep, blocked his way. Stunned, Warren climbed the face of the pile until he reached the top, some seventy-five feet above the path.

"It's gone," he whispered to himself. "Christ, they're buried alive." As far as his light would penetrate the darkness, he could see only black rock rubble. The night was silent once again. Only the wind now made any sound.

Warren turned and retraced his steps down the rock face to the path. He turned for a moment in disbelief at the sight, then slowly climbed back up the hill to the radio outpost.

Inside, Lynn had found some clothing and had managed to light the oil lamp by the time Warren returned. She still looked pale.

"War, what's down there?"

She could tell by his expression it was bad.

"I don't know exactly. There's been a rock slide or something. I can't see any buildings. I think a lot of them are buried, Lynn. I just don't know." He sat down beside her and noticed that she was shivering. Searching around, he found her sleeping bag and spread it out on the bunk.

"Get some sleep, hon. We can't do anything until it gets light." He pulled some blankets around himself and dozed off.

Because of the northern latitude, it was late morning before there was enough light, though both Lynn and Warren had been up for several hours trying to restore some order to the outpost. The steel building, flexible in its construction, had survived with only minor damage: the door would not close and one window was smashed, along with a toppled stovepipe. Warren's main concern was for the radio equipment; he could not tell how much damage the units had suffered.

"It's horrible, War. We've got to try to find them," Lynn said as they faced the rock slide at the base of the hill. Half of the mountainside had spread out across the valley, leaving a huge scar on the mountain face. The black rock lay in sharp contrast to the snow.

They made their way slowly across the top. As far as they could see, the blackness covered Stongsfjörd.

"Let's head for the harbor. If anyone survived, they would be there. If the slide went into the fjord—." Warren didn't finish. The thought chilled him.

"I hear something, War, over this way!" Lynn started to run.

"Be careful!" Warren yelled after her, but to no avail. She had disappeared down the slope. When Warren caught up with her she was talking with two women and a man, the sole survivors of Stongsfjörd.

The Strathers family, Peter, Melinda, and their daughter Sara, lived in the last unit before the harbor. Now only the front half was exposed, the rear buried in rubble. Beyond, the harbor lay clear, the overturned hull of the ship still as it had been since the sinking. Peter Strathers, an Australian, was speaking in hushed tones to Lynn.

"It all happened in a few seconds. We heard the awful roar and ran outside. Our unit was shaking terribly. It was all over so fast! We heard the screams, but there was nothing to do." He pointed to the rock face. "They're all under there, God rest their souls."

"We were at the outpost. It's still in one piece," Lynn explained. Then almost apologetically, she said, "You're welcome to join us."

They picked up what clothing could be rescued from the half-buried living unit and made their way slowly back across the slide area. They were silent during the trek out of respect for those whose grave would forever be the mass of rock beneath their feet.

"You found no one?" Warren asked of Peter once they had reached the path to the outpost.

"No, they're all down—there," was his reply.

Warren and Lynn knew very little about the Strathers family. Peters had been an Anglican circuit priest in the Australian outback, and for reasons unknown had joined the Stongsfjörd effort. His wife, Melinda, was slight. Her face and hands showed the signs of hard labor, yet her eyes were soft and kind. She spoke perfect English, the kind taught in private schools in the Commonwealth. Sara was tall. She had the dark wavy hair of her father, and her eyes flashed. She had a fighting spirit, more so than either of her parents. Peter had held church services for those who wished to attend at Stongsfjörd. Since he was a knowledgeable horticulturist, he had also been involved with the greenhouse project. That effort had saved their lives; he had moved his family next to the harbor so that he would be closer to the greenhouse site.

The five survivors of the Stongsfjörd slide climbed the slope to the outpost. Below, all was quiet save for a few screaming sea gulls who seemed perplexed by the sudden change in topography.

"The inside took a beating," Warren commented as they approached the building, "but I think we can make room inside for all of us. The rear storeroom is empty—you're welcome to use it."

"I'm sure it will serve. You are most kind." Melinda was grateful for any shelter.

Inside they rearranged the food stores to provide extra room, and Warren spent the remainder of the day on the radio. Peter, handy as a carpenter, reset the stove and patched the broken windows. He fitted the door so once again the building was secure against the cold. The steam line had been severed in the quake, but Peter was able to make a patch using a piece of tin and some rocks. Gradually the outpost began to warm up. The three women salvaged as much of the kitchen equipment as possible. By early evening, the interior was livable and their thoughts turned to supper.

"The food stores here are all that we have. We will share them," Lynn said casually. There really was no other alternative. Peter seemed to understand her thoughts. "You have made a great sacrifice for us. Thanks."

Peter gave the blessing, and the five ate mostly in silence. They were still strangers to each other, but time would erase the barriers.

16. Reunion

Warren worked into the night on the radio equipment trying to get at least one of the receivers operational. The batteries and generator seemed to be undamaged, so as long as the fuel supply held out, there was still the chance of making radio contact. More than ever Warren wanted to contact Charlie and Gus; this time he would reveal his identity.

All that would have to wait until tomorrow, though, because the Strathers were exhausted from their ordeal and needed sleep. Several times during the night Warren thought he felt the building shake, but it was only the wind blowing hard and cold against the walls.

By midmorning the next day, Warren felt that he had the radio ready to go on the air. Peter watched him as the set crackled into life. Their only contact with the outside world was alive.

Checking the logbook, Warren got on Charlie's frequency and sent the call.

"Sand Cay, this is Solar III."

That ought to wake them up! It sure as hell did. Charlie's voice came back loud and clear.

"Solar III, this is Sand Cay—identify—repeat, identify!"

Warren laughed. "Warren Belting, Stongsfjörd, Ice."

For a moment after that Charlie and Gus both tried to speak, and then Charlie got through.

"Are you okay? Do you know anything about Lynn?"

"She is here with me. All okay. Earthquake yesterday. Only five of us left here now. Not much food."

Charlie came back, "Give me your location, Warren."

Warren passed the information on to Charlie, and there was silence for a moment.

Then, "Warren, have you any runway capability. How about housing?"

Warren replied, "There's one strip thirty-six hundred feet northeast-southwest on two-foot compacted snow. One building left, but a lot of construction materials; could build more."

Gus came on for the reply. "We have a plane, food, and maybe enough fuel to get to you. Our island taking a beating with the storms. Don't know how long this house will take it. We will consider flight plans after we check fuel. Will call you twenty hundred hours your time. Out."

Warren cut the power to save fuel and turned to see the Strathers staring at him; they were obviously puzzled. Warren looked at Lynn. She nodded, so he started from the beginning with Solar III. There was no reason to hold anything back. In fact, it was a relief to share the secret with someone else.

Peter was the first to speak. "What a horrible experience. You are lucky to have been spared, what with your government and all that."

Sara looked at Warren. "What are our chances?" she asked. "Will it ever stop?"

"I don't know," he replied. "The Solar disturbance may go on for years, or end tomorrow. Without any data from the satellite, we can't tell."

"Perhaps," Peter mused, "it is the end of the world, Judgment Day."

At eight o'clock, the five at Stongsfjörd gathered around the radio set for the transmittal from Sand Cay. Charlie's voice filled the room.

"Ice—how do you hear?"

Warren grabbed the mike. "Loud and clear, Sand Cay. How about me?"

"Okay, Ice, we are going to make a try at it. Leave here tomorrow early. Can't give you much of an E.T.A.—don't know how fast this crate will run. Mark your runway with an arrow and hot your radio twenty hours from sign off. Over."

"Okay, Charlie. Good luck. Out."

Warren turned to the group—"We'll have to make room for two guests."

The next day, they worked to salvage as much as they could in the way of belongings from the ruins of the Strathers' unit. The extra bedding would come in handy for Charlie and Gus.

A tour of the greenhouse and power plant sites completed the day's work. The greenhouses could be repaired, and there was plenty of wood and sheet metal at the power plant to build an addition to the outpost. If Charlie and Gus could make it with the food, they could survive. Without additional supplies, they had at the most two months' stores in the outpost. Two months was not very long.

"I wonder why they picked Sand Cay?" Lynn asked.

"Probably their only choice. Houston and D.C. were burning and they had to get out. The Cay used to be the practice target for the radar crews. Not much out there except the old house and control tower. Sort of a lonesome place, I would think." Warren knew Charlie liked to be with people. Island life was not his style—at least, not an island the size of or as barren as Sand Cay.

They cleared a large arrow on the runway, the dark asphalt contrasting with the snow. The landing lights should pick it up. Beyond that, all they could do was to start the generator and keep the radio set on.

Within half an hour of their stated arrival time, Charlie's voice filled the room: "Ice, this is Sand Cay, identify."

Warren grabbed the mike—"Loud and clear, Charlie. Where the hell are you?"

There was a pause, then, "Okay, Ice, we got a fix. We're about twenty minutes from touchdown—any weather?"

"No, Charlie, wind northeast at fifteen, and two feet of compacted snow on top. Be careful with your gear; don't stub your toe." Warren was afraid of the nose landing gear. It could dig in and collapse in the touchdown.

Charlie came back, "We'll keep her tail down as long as we can. Keep in contact. We will make one pass to look things over."

The sound of the approaching plane was eerie. They had become so used to the quiet of Stongsfjörd. Soon the landing lights came on, and the old cargo plane made one pass, low over the strip. Charlie was on the radio.

"Okay, we got you. We're coming in!"

The plane circled low and let down, against the wind. They touched with the nose high and fishtailed down the runway, slowly dropping the nose. The front gear dug in hard, collapsing the strut, and the plane nosed into the ground, grinding to a halt. Five figures ran in hot pursuit down the runway. Charlie and Gus had arrived!

When they reached the aircraft, Charlie had already opened the cargo hatch and was attempting to lower a ramp. The angle of the plane made the task difficult.

He called out to them. "Give me a hand. Gus is hurt!"

Warren and Peter grabbed the lower edge of the ramp and pulled themselves into the cargo hold. It was dark except for the red emergency-exit lights.

"Up here."

Charlie led them forward to the cockpit, where they saw Gus's form slumped over the controls.

"He hit the panel when we pitched. I tied part of my shirt around his head—he's bleeding bad."

Warren stopped for a moment, grabbed Charlie's shoulders, and gripped him hard.

"Good to see you—this is Peter Strathers. Peter, Charlie Richardson."

They quickly carried Gus back to the cargo hatch and lowered him down the ramp. Using a blanket as a makeshift stretcher, the group made their way through the snow to the outpost. Inside, they lay him on the bunk nearest the stove. Sara seemed to know what to do and took over.

"Lynn and I will take care of the gentleman. Please bring any medical supplies you have with you in the plane."

"Come on, Warren," Charlie called. "There's an emergency kit in the plane."

The two headed back down the slope to the abandoned aircraft, its landing lights still shining across the snow-covered field. Inside, they found a large case marked "medical supplies, emergency use only." Charlie paused long enough to switch the power off. They felt their way back to the hatch in total darkness.

Sara opened the case and searched through the contents.

"Bring over that boiling water so we can get this stuff sterile."

She filled the syringe with a sedative and, with the speed of a professional, gave Gus the injection. She then carefully unwrapped the cloth around his head, wrung out a towel in the hot water, and cleansed the wound. She applied a sterile dressing from the medical supplies and dressed the wound in gauze. Gus was still unconscious, though his breathing was regular. Sara wrapped him in blankets and pulled a chair over beside the bunk. She was determined to save him.

"I'll watch him for a while. You people better get some sleep."

Charlie sat up with Sara and Gus for a while, but the fatigue of the flight took its toll. He pulled a sleeping bag over by the stove and was soon fast asleep. Outside, the air was still and cold.

Gus showed no change throughout the next day. Sara slept briefly in the morning, but kept by his side.

The three men assembled a makeshift sled and transferred the food supplies from the plane to the outpost. The cases were certainly a welcome sight. Their own supplies would have been exhausted by midsummer. Tomorrow, they would strip the aircraft of the radio equipment to replace that damaged in the earthquake.

"How is our patient doing, Sara?" Peter asked as he entered the outpost for the evening meal.

"Much the same, Father. I hope he will come around soon."

Peter looked at Gus; he guessed him to be about forty or so. He had the lean frame of the military man. Peter had Gus in his prayers now—this man who had come from America should live; there were so few left now.

Peter's prayers were answered the following morning when Gus opened his eyes and asked, "What's going on?"

During his recovery, Gus was assigned to the radio, and once again contact was established with the remaining groups throughout the world. Stongsfjörd was not the only area to be destroyed by an earthquake; there had been many throughout the world. Nearby, Reykjavik had suffered major damage, while the west coast of America had been hit with a series of quakes. Hawaii's volcanoes were active, and it was rumored that the presidential retreat had been destroyed. No one knew if the executive party had survived or not. Rome and much of southern Italy had also been badly damaged. Several flag pins on the wall map were changed to black, since some of the stations no longer responded to a call.

It was another week before Gus could walk unassisted or venture outside. Sara continued to stay with him, and Peter had decided that his daughter's intentions were more than simply medical. He was fifteen years her senior, but when time was measured in months of food supplies, years did not seem to matter much. Sara had never had much of a social life; the Australian outback demanded most of one's time for simple existence. Once when she had been on holiday with a friend in Melbourne, the large city was too much of a change and she had returned home early. The outback had its virtues: peace, a rugged outdoor existence, and it produced in one a deep appreciation for living things. Survival itself was a way of life, and Sara carried that will to survive with her even here.

Before Sara was born, Peter had been the parish priest of a large Anglican church in Melbourne. His future seemed secure, but then the scandal intervened. He had been accused of using collection money illegally for his own expenses. Even though later he was vindicated, the stories haunted him, and the outback was a refuge from flapping tongues. His faith increased as he combined God's will to survive with his own.

One evening after the meal, Sara asked Gus to share the story of Solar III with her parents. He told of Warren and Lynn's involvement and the false charges lodged against them by the government after their flight into Mexico. Gus also related the exposé by Senator Johnson and the subsequent rapid deterioration of the governmental system. Then the waves of panic, followed by the looting and burning of the cities. Sand Cay had been their last resort when they knew Houston was doomed. There was no military or civilian command left in the United States. The President and his advisors had retreated to Hawaii, leaving the country in shambles.

"Panic," Gus concluded. "Panic was what destroyed America. I'm still convinced that if order could have been maintained, the country might have survived. What amazes me was the short time involved in our collapse. We gave up without a real fight."

Sara answered him, "Yet we are here, alive, and fight we will." She put her arm around Gus. "We have to do what we can. At least we have food and each other."

Peter interrupted her. "We have much to thank the Lord for. Let's be content with what we have and what we can do."

Charlie took Warren aside after Gus had finished.

"About Sally. You should know."

Warren looked at him. "Know what, Charlie?"

"Sally was involved in an attempt to take over the Houston base, Warren. She lost her life in the try."

Charlie decided not to detail the episode any more than to let Warren know of her fate. Warren said nothing for a moment, then he turned to Charlie.

"Thanks. I'm glad it's over for her and that we know. Thanks, Charlie."

Warren returned to the group with Charlie. He sat down beside Lynn and grasped her hand.

"War, anything wrong?" she asked softly.

"It's okay. I'll tell you later, hon."

"Tomorrow," Peter said as he turned down the lantern, "we will bring some of those panels up from the terminal plant site and build on to this place."

The west mountain coast of Mexico, usually a warm tropical paradise for the well-to-do tourist, was snow-covered and cold. The ocean, dark and whipped by the wind, beat upon the beaches usually filled with the bikini set. Except for one hotel, the resort community of El Sora Vi was empty. The single hotel was ablaze with lights, and music mingled with laughter filled the air, competing with the howl of the surf. Inside was Wallace Redding's retreat, a haven unique in the world. Based on Weld Smith's information, Redding had filled the building with food, supplies, and a wealthy clientele willing to pay the price of one million dollars each for survival. Even Weld Smith, bailed out of D.C. by Redding's "advisors," was in attendance. The affair had all the attributes of a twenty-four-hour bash. Solar III was for only the poor to face.

"Just think, man," Wallace said to Weld. "When all those bastards die off, think of all that land!"

Weld was pleased with the idea. "We can run things our way for a change. Reckon we won't have to listen to all those bastards every time we want to do something! Why, Texas could be the whole world!"

Weld liked the feeling of power. He was at the top now. All of the D.C. work was paying off.

"Hey, Weld." Wallace interrupted his thoughts. "Why don't we try some skiing tomorrow? Take some broads along and, if we get a little cold on the slopes, they can warm us up!"

"Yeah, sounds good," Weld replied. He wondered where Redding got all his energy. Christ, the man must be seventy, and he still lived for booze, broads, and bucks.

"Say, Weld," Redding called, "ya'll know whatever happened to that bastard, Johnson? God I hope he's dead!"

Weld could hardly hear him above the din of the party.

"Don't know, W.C. Maybe he burned up in the D.C. fire."

Redding didn't answer directly. He looked into his cocktail glass and said, "Christ, it's empty again." He left Weld and headed over to the bar.

The wind let up during the night and the sun was out by midmorning, clear and still cold. Weld looked out of his suite window and regretted the skiing agreement the night before. Yet if W.C. wanted to ski, that is exactly what they would do.

As he put his feet on the floor to get out of bed, he felt a strange tremble. By the time he reached the bathroom, the drinking glasses on the counter were rattling, and Weld could feel the sway of the building.

"God! A quake!" Weld grabbed his bathrobe and rushed into the hall. It was already jammed with guests. People were screaming. He could hear the sound of broken glass.

Slowly at first, then gaining speed, the mountainside began to move downward toward the beach, carrying the hotel with it, still upright. The mass of rock moved, almost floating, out across the floor of the sea. Weld saw for an instant water—and then darkness.

The beaches of El Sora Vi were covered with the rock now. There would never be any more sand, sun, and bikinis. The empire of W. D. Redding was buried under sixty feet of water and four hundred thousand tons of rock.

The sea lapped against its new shoreline, starting again the geologic conversion to sand. The sun was hidden by an immense cloud of dust.

17.
Contact

Bumper Johnson looked out over the snow-covered landscape of Vermont. He'd started to write a record of the events of Solar III, but he had lost interest. He found himself more interested in the present and the future. Bumper put his papers away for the moment and turned his attention to the coming evening's town meeting.

Senator Johnson had organized weekly town meetings as a way of exchanging information and planning their survival activities. It gave the people involved something to do other than worry about the state of things. Using an antenna wired inside the church steeple, radio communications had also been established with a few other isolated groups, and, as with Stongsfjörd, a record was kept of the contacts.

The town had seen only two visitors. First a man, half crazy with terror, had somehow made the trip from New York City, and then a stray beagle dog had been found by Mrs. Boardman. Sherri had nursed the dog back to health, but the man was not as fortunate. He died from exposure three days after his arrival. Before his passing, he related what he had left behind. New York City was gutted by the fires. The buildings stood, empty, tall, and black against the sky. The dead were first bulldozed into piles and burned. Later, they were left to decay on the streets. Some, who stayed, took to killing and eating the rats which fed on the rotting corpses. Finally, there were acts of cannibalism. Hundreds of thousands tried to leave the city—on foot, for the most part. The throughways were lined with the bodies of those who had tried. As the snow fell, white mounds marked the dead. He had lived by taking food from the dead, many of whom had tried to carry some provisions with them.

Tent camps had been set up by those lucky enough to have that means of shelter, though he'd seen many such camps abandoned as food and fuel ran out. When asked how many people were left in New York City, the poor man formed the letter "O" with his thumb and forefinger. They buried him in the churchyard.

As the radio contacts increased, Bumper tried to estimate the number of world survivors. Their radio could not reach the Far East, so the tallies included Europe only. That continent had not fared any better than the U.S. All of their major cities had been destroyed.

About half of the contacts were lost during the "week of the quakes," as the series of disasters was termed by Bumper's group. All of the volcanoes in the Hawaiian Islands became active, and confirmation came that the President and his executive staff had perished. Vermont was fortunate to be positioned on some of the earth's oldest and most stable rock. There had been tremors, but no damage. There were reports that the West Coast of the Americas had been virtually destroyed with the shifting of the massive San Andreas fault. They had lost their only contact in San Francisco and were unable to confirm any of the reports. Bumper often wondered what would come next—disease? Even the return of the continental ice sheets was a possibility.

As the calendar at least signaled spring, Senator Johnson urged the town to draft some uniform laws for mutual survival. With no growing season, feed for the animals would soon be depleted and a starving cow was of no use to anyone. Thus the animals would be slaughtered and the meat consumed first. Staples such as grain and potatoes would be preserved for later use. The meat of course would not keep.

Wood-cutting crews were assigned the task of supplying fuel for those unable to cut for themselves. In several cases, many people were moved into a single home to conserve heat. Medical supplies were stored in the town hall, and in an emergency that building would serve as a hospital. After much discussion, it was decided that strangers would be cared for only with the consent of the entire group. Food supplies were limited, and disease brought in by a stranger could wipe out the entire community. There were no laws now—they had to make their own.

Bumper liked to listen to the radio calls; it was comforting to know that others were still alive in the rest of the world. Their nearest "neighbor" to the south was the village of Applewood, some 150 miles distant. Eleven people had managed to survive thus far. Bumper was in contact with them when the Applewood transmitter was interrupted for a moment. When it returned to life, the voice was excited.

"Bumper, we have word that a large group of survivors in New York have formed an army. They're pretty tough—rob and kill everything in their path. We've been told that they are coming up the river road, headed our way. Better prepare yourselves."

"Thanks, Applewood. We will call you tomorrow. Out."

Bumper turned to the half dozen people who had been listening.

One old man bristled, "Hell, I'll sure fight before they get me!"

Others mumbled approval as Bumper turned to them.

"We will meet here tonight. Pass the word—get everyone!" The hall emptied quickly, Bumper pulled on his coat and boots and headed up the road to the farm.

Inside, the warmth felt good; the cold left Bumper for the moment. He called the group together and told them of the radio transmission.

"We're going to meet tonight and call them again. We'd better think of something if that mob is headed this way."

John got a county map from the desk and spread it on the kitchen table.

"Here," he said pointing to the road. "They will have to come up the valley to reach us from Applewood. Over here's Carpenter Creek Reservoir. Now if we could bust all that ice and water loose, I figure that would stop the mob, right?"

Bumper thought for a moment. "One problem, John. It would also hit Applewood, I'm afraid."

John nodded. "Yeah, I didn't think of that. You're right."

They put the map aside in preparation for dinner.

That night Bumper called the meeting to order and explained the threat of the mob. As the group began to talk all at once, he banged the gavel.

"We will try to contact Applewood now for an update. Quiet, please!"

Applewood crackled. "Bumper, we've spotted them. Damn, there must be hundreds. I have to leave, I'll leave the mike on. Good luck." For the next half hour only background noise came through; then the sound of shots. There were yells and screams, then silence as the radio set was either destroyed or turned off.

Bumper was the first to speak. "We're next, unless we stop them somehow. It'll take them a day to get up here from Applewood."

John raised his hand. "Senator Johnson," he asked, "now what about Carpenter Creek Dam? It's our only hope; Applewood didn't have a chance."

The group seemed stunned until a man in the rear spoke up.

"I have some dynamite left over from blowing stumps; you're welcome to use it. I think Mr. Boardman is right. It is our only chance to survive."

The next morning, two figures made their way up the ravine towards the reservoir and Carpenter Creek Dam: John Boardman and Andrew Jacobs, the man with the dynamite. Andrew knew the trade. He had worked as a blaster in a quarry for thirty-two years. His skill and John's strength made up the team. Between them they had more than a hundred pounds of explosives and Andrew's old blasting machine. On snowshoes, the trip was agonizing and slow. It took until noon for them to make the spillway.

In the village, an observer had stationed himself in the church steeple where he could spot any movement in the valley along the river. He would wait until the mob approached the mouth of Carpenter's Creek, and then he would fire two shots from his double-barreled shotgun.

Andrew and John placed the charges at the base of the spillway gates and wired the detonators, using two for each charge. Andrew was afraid that the detonators were too old to be reliable. He knew his work, John thought, as they ran the wires up to the blasting machine. Andrew had replaced the handle with a flat board. He first raised the board and placed an empty beer bottle between the underside of the board and the top of the blasting machine. He then placed a large boulder on top of the board. He turned to John.

"Hope you're a good shot with that rifle."

John nodded, and they attached the wires to the terminals on the blasting machine. Andrew made one last inspection of his handiwork. Satisfied, he motioned to John.

"Let's get out of here. If that bottle breaks—"

High on the ridge, John placed one round in the old single-shot Winchester lever-action rifle, found a boulder for a steady rest, and, with Andrew, waited. Thirty minutes later, two shots were heard up the valley.

"That's it, John. Be careful."

John held his breath and squeezed off the round; the bullet glanced off the boulder on top of the blasting machine.

"Too high, John. Pull down, m'boy," Andrew urged. John reloaded, aimed, and fired again.

A terrific explosion rocked the entire valley as the spillway and floodgates gave way, followed by a wall of ice and water fifty feet high. Andrew and John watched, petrified with excitement, as the wall advanced down the ravine and into the valley. It hit the mob as a wave twenty feet high and half a mile wide. Applewood would be their last victim. The water spread out into a large, shallow lake, its black surface covering the dead. Andrew and John headed over the top of the ridge and back to the village. They did not look behind them.

That evening, Bumper joined the small group at the hall to listen to the radio. Some of the others were celebrating, but somehow Bumper did not feel in the mood for revelry. It was like a civil war over food. Less than a year ago, those who had just died were ordinary citizens of New York City.

The radio operator interrupted his thoughts. "Senator, I've got an odd one. Some Americans broadcasting from Iceland. Come listen."

The contact was fairly clear now. "This is Ice. Can you hear?"

Bumper picked up the mike. "Yes, loud and clear. Are you American?"

Gus's voice answered, "Affirmative."

Bumper continued the questioning. "What part of America?" The answer came back, "Washington, D.C., and Houston, Texas." *How the hell did they get to Iceland,* Bumper wondered.

"Identify, please," Bumper replied.

"Gustav Olsson," came the reply.

"Senator Johnson here," Bumper replied. The next transmission brought him to his feet.

"Not the Senator Johnson who blew the whistle on Solar III by any chance?"

For the next half hour, Bumper never left the transmitter. It was incredible that these people, who had been involved in the project from the start, were still alive.

They asked if Bumper knew anything about the fate of Houston, Texas. Other than the fire, Bumper knew nothing. They compared radio contacts. In the continental U.S., Bumper had only thirty-four remaining, none in any major city. In turn, Gus could offer little information as to the fate of Iceland. They had seen no one, but with the snow and cold one could hardly expect travelers. Gus also passed European data on to Bumper.

"With all that expertise over there," Bumper asked, "how long is this thing going to last?"

Gus's answer was short. "Beats me. It had better let up before we run out of food, though."

It was getting late. The day for Bumper had been long and tiring. He signed off, shut the generator down, and headed back to the farm. He did not stop to look at the valley of destruction behind him.

During the weeks that followed, John made several trips down the valley toward Applewood to look for survivors and salvage. He found nothing but mid-sized and massive cakes of ice. The path of the flood was outlined where mud met snow. Slowly, new snow covered the scar, and the event was only a memory.

Since the initial radio contact, Stongsfjörd had kept in daily communication with Bumper's group. A separate wing had been added to the outpost so that those on radio watch did not disturb the others; it also allowed some privacy for the couples. It was during one of their turns at the radio that Warren had told Lynn about Sally. She liked Sally, what little she knew of her, but had wondered how Sally and Warren ever managed to get married; they seemed so completely opposite to each other.

"I'm sorry, War. It sounds funny, but I am sorry." They never mentioned the subject again.

Peter at first honored the sabbath with his family alone, but he was pleased as time passed to share his faith with the others. Sara initially brought Gus into the fold, followed by Charlie, and finally Warren and Lynn. They began to reserve Sunday evening for such gatherings, and discussions generally followed Peter's service.

Gus was the first to broach the subject.

"Peter, if what you believe in is true, how do you account for what has happened to us—to the earth, for that matter?"

Peter didn't answer for some time. Then he spoke very quietly. "Sometimes the reasons for our Lord's actions are not made clear to us. We are asked to rely on faith. I, for one, have faith that there will be another year, another world, just as in Australia we had to have faith when the drought destroyed the crops. It is a matter of waiting, not being impatient, and being faithful." Peter had the ability to join people together for their common good; he was a real asset to Stongsfjörd.

Faith was becoming increasingly important to Lynn. She had suspected, and now was certain, that she was pregnant. She had not told Warren as yet; she was almost afraid to talk about it to him. Lynn had made up her mind on one point, though; she wanted to be married before the child was born.

After the contact with Senator Johnson, the Americans began to think of returning eventually to their homeland for whatever time was left to them. They wished to be home. Charlie brought the subject up one evening after their meal.

"Peter, I guess you would like to return to Australia sometime, but would you consider America?"

Peter laughed. "I've not minded living with you Yanks. We're all in this kettle together. Don't rightly see how we can leave this shack right now, though."

Gus picked up the conversation. "We flew that crate in here; we could fly it out. I don't know what all we damaged coming in, but it's worth a look if we want to leave."

The expressions on their faces gave the answer. Home, if there was a way!

The following day Gus and Charlie surveyed the plane's condition. The broken nose-wheel strut was the worst problem, because the hydraulic cylinder was damaged beyond repair.

Fuel would have to be carried from the supply dump at the thermal site to the plane—not an impossible task, but traversing a mile in the cold with the snow would be miserable work. Yet it could be done. All the food would also have to be reloaded aboard.

That evening they made contact with Bumper and asked if there was an airfield nearby in usable condition.

"You folks sure like to fly around don't you?" the Senator commented. "It's midnight here. Let us look around tomorrow and call you. There was something down toward Applewood, but our flood may have washed it out. Have your set on at eight P.M. your time."

Gus closed him out and turned to the group. "We'd best do some looking too!"

There was a good deal of activity at Stongsfjörd the next day. Peter got one of the crawler tractors running at the construction site while the others built a sled to transport drums of fuel to the aircraft. Warren located a spare hydraulic cylinder for the tractor that looked as if it might serve as a replacement for the damaged landing gear. It would take at least a month's effort, but there was a good chance they could be airborne.

They eagerly awaited the call from Vermont. If only Bumper's group had a landing site available. The call came exactly at eight.

"Ice, this is Vermont station. How do you hear?"

"Clear, Senator, go ahead!" replied Charlie.

Bumper came back: "We don't have much to offer, but the county airport landing field is still intact. We can talk you down with our radio and light some fires to outline the runway. We'd sure like to see you make the trip."

Charlie called back: "Senator, we think we can fix this crate and get it off the ground, but we will be a month getting ready. It's better than sitting on this hill waiting to die."

After they signed off, Lynn put her arm around Warren.

"Can we stay and talk for a little while, War?" He nodded, holding her hand.

"War," she continued. "War, we are going to be parents. I'm sure I'm pregnant."

He sat up rigid for a moment and looked at her in disbelief.

"You're certain?" he whispered.

"Yes, hon, I am," was her reply. "And, War, I'd like our child to have a mother and father. I mean, I'd like Peter to marry us."

It was almost too much for him: first a baby and now marriage. He had never told Lynn that, because of Sally's fear of childbirth, he had been surgically sterilized shortly after their marriage. Warren could not possibly be the father of Lynn's child, and yet who else? They had been together constantly at Stongsfjörd—she had appeared to be so faithful. Well, at any rate, whoever it was must be buried under the slide.

She sensed that something was wrong. "War, I love you. You are the only person I have ever loved this way. I just feel that we should be part of Peter's faith, especially now."

He didn't understand at all. But he did love her. Something inside him urged him to be patient, and understanding would come later. Warren held her close.

"Yes," he said, almost without realizing it. "We will."

The repairs to the plane and the preparations for the return to America under ordinary circumstances would have taken only a few days, but with the cold and the short daylight hours, minor tasks seemed endless.

First, a wood-timber frame was constructed under the nose of the aircraft and the plane jacked up and leveled. Only then could the front gear be dismantled and reassembled using the new hydraulic cylinder. Charlie serviced the engines as best he could, also inspecting the control equipment. The generator set from the outpost was altered to charge the aircraft batteries and to supply electricity for cabin lights. Gradually, though, the aircraft regained its image as something that might fly. With the progress, the group's morale improved as well. It was an important event when at last Charlie and Gus spooled up the engines for a test and the old plane almost shivered in expectation of flight.

After the food and fuel were stowed aboard, Peter brought the crawler tractor over from the construction site to clear snow from the runway. That task alone took two days to complete. In some areas, drifts six feet deep had accumulated.

The day before the departure attempt, the outpost called all of their radio contacts and told them that Stongsfjörd was closing out. They would re-establish contact from America. The stations wished the group good luck.

Peter spent that last evening in prayer. Indeed, had the Lord not said, "I will be with you until the end of the earth"? Peter felt that they were very close to the end. As usual, he placed his trust in the Almighty and slept peacefully that last night.

Prior to departure, Gus made their last contact with Bumper in Vermont. He gave them an estimated time of arrival and got assurances from Bumper that their runway was clear and that fires would be burning at either end to act as markers. They would also keep in constant radio contact. Gus signed off, and the radio gear was placed aboard the plane.

The Icelandic dawn witnessed a strange sight and sound: a lone plane, engines at full throttle, lumbered along a black gravel path, gaining speed and finally becoming airborne. The aircraft made one circle over Stongsfjörd and then headed out over the fjord, westward. Below was silence. A small cross at the base of the rock slide marked the grave of those who would stay forever. The sound of the plane was lost in the wind.

Flying without any navigation aids reminded Charlie of the early days of World War II. Often one had to fly without radio contact to avoid detection by the enemy.

The weather was clear until they reached the Grand Banks. Then a heavy cloud cover began to form. Gus called Bumper about their weather.

"Looks like it might snow. Sorry to say that it's overcast here now. You must be two hours out yet."

Gus looked at his watch. They should make it by daylight.

Charlie looked over at Gus, who was also looking alternately at the clouds and the fuel gauges.

"Gus, we've got to drop down to see where we are."

"Yeah, Charlie, I know, but there are mountains down there and I don't know how low that cover's hanging." Gus turned to the rest of the group. "Hang on. We're going to take a look."

They dropped through the cover for what seemed like an endless time. When they broke through, Gus had barely enough time to avoid hitting the wooded slope of a mountain.

"No good," he said. "We're going back up."

He put the plane into a steep climb until they cleared the cloud cover. Then Gus turned to Charlie.

"See if you can get a fix on Johnson's radio. We can't stay up here forever."

Charlie did the best he could with the radio equipment on board, but his error factor was still at least fifty miles. He passed the data to Gus.

"We still have to get under this. They might be able to hear our engines."

Gus nodded and searched the horizon for signs of clear sky; there was none.

Peter sensed the urgency of the problem and came forward to the cockpit.

"Anything I can do for you chaps?" he asked.

"Yeah," answered Charlie. "Pray for a hole in that soup below us." He spoke half in jest.

Peter looked out over the clouds and, in his way, asked for help. His mind seemed to be almost taken from him for a moment, and then something told him to look out the port side of the aircraft. Below, to his amazement, it was clear; the snow-covered hills of Vermont lay directly beneath.

"Gus!" Peter called. "Off your port wing."

Gus had already seen the hole and put the aircraft into a steep bank for the descent. As they dropped, the cloud cover filled in above them, and they leveled off at 2500 feet, headed south down a long valley. Peter gave his thanks—yet while he was in wonder of it all, his prayers were interrupted by the radio. Bumper could hear them! They were north of the field.

Within five minutes, the fires came into view, and Gus turned to the group.

"Hook up! We're coming home!"

He let the plane down for the approach. As the wheels touched the runway, the sky had darkened and snow was falling. A lone figure with a team and sleigh witnessed the arrival. John Boardman breathed a sign of relief as the plane taxied toward him. He was amazed that they had located the field in such bad weather.

18. Home

The farm was cheerful that evening, filled with happy voices and laughter. For a few hours, the torment of the weather was forgotten and the talk was of old times, before "it" happened.

The farmhouse was full now. Tomorrow they would unload the plane and store the food supplies. Tonight before he retired, Peter remembered again the promise: "Yea, till the end of the world I will be with you." How else could the events of the landing have occurred? His wife was already asleep as he climbed into an honest-to-goodness old-fashioned bed and pulled the warm covers over him.

A week of effort was spent in moving the supplies from the plane to the potato bins on the Boardman farm. They tied and blocked the plane, without fuel now. It had made its last flight. Soon the snow would cover the wings and fuselage, making it all but invisible. Once again, the radio equipment was removed and added to the village hall set.

Senator Johnson called a meeting to introduce the new arrivals. He did not mention their relationship with Solar III, saying only that they were technicians stranded in Iceland. They had brought their own food and would be no burden on the rest of the group.

News of the world was discussed, with the exception of Russia and China. The condition was much the same: ruined cities, isolated small groups of survivors, and no change in the weather. Attempts to establish radio contact in those two countries had failed. One could only assume that their plight was that of the rest of the world.

Without any sign of spring, cattle feed would soon be running low, and plans were continued to slaughter the animals for food.

Many of the wild animals faced the same fate. Without spring foliage, they too would not last far into the "summer." A few domestic animals would be spared for breeding stock, if the world returned to normal. The herds could be rebuilt. The community would now survive only on the resources at hand.

Warren and Lynn asked Peter to talk to them together about a month after they arrived at the farm. They told him of their past and their desire to be married. Lynn also added that she was expecting a baby. Peter had been faced with the same situation many times in the outback of Australia. Often a couple just couldn't wait for the preacher's semiannual visit. His sorrow was with the child; what chance for survival was there? Yet children would be born until the last couple on earth perished. How could he, Peter, be the judge?

"You have my prayers and my blessings," he concluded.

Bumper was pleased with the renewed activity around the farm. It took his mind away from the past events, and with the physical work, he actually felt better than he had in years. He was concerned about Mrs. Boardman, however. She seemed to be failing somewhat. Perhaps it was all the extra work, though everyone helped. She had lost weight, and often retired early ahead of the others. Finally Bumper spoke to Peter about her.

"She won't own up to anything being wrong, but perhaps you can talk to her. She's done so much for us all."

"I'll try," Peter replied. "I've noticed something, too."

The group was without a doctor, which added to the potential danger of any illness. Also, a disease could spread to others unchecked. Peter found an opportunity to speak with Mrs. Boardman the next evening.

"Are you all right? You seem to favor your right side." He'd noticed her slight limp.

She blushed as she spoke. "Old age, I guess, Father; hits all of us sooner or later, and what with this terrible winter without end." She changed the subject and the matter was dropped until the next morning—when she didn't get up at all.

Sherri was calling, "Peter come quick; it's Mom!" Peter was just starting down the stairs for breakfast. He turned and ran to Mrs.

Boardman's room. The lady lay pale; her breathing was shallow and her hands cold.

"What is it?" Peter asked Sherri.

"She has a tumor—her right side. I think there's a lot of pain. Please, Peter, can't we do something for her?"

"Call Lynn and Sara," he replied. "They at least can try to make her comfortable." He waited until the two arrived, then left the women alone.

The day passed quietly, with Mrs. Boardman near death by nightfall. They could not operate to relieve the pressure. It was only a matter of time for her. John was taking it hard.

"Is this what is left for us?" he asked the group after supper. "We're all to die one by one till there's no one left?"

"Please, John," Peter answered. "We're doing all that we can for your mother. What has happened to her is not of our doing. You shouldn't blame anyone."

The matter did bother Peter, though. The greater meaning of the entire experience escaped him. But his faith told him to serve his Lord until the end, and that he would do.

After the others had retired, Peter went up to Mrs. Boardman's room. Sherri was with her. Mrs. Boardman had become "mom" to Sherri; the two had gotten along like mother and daughter from the start. Sherri stayed for a few minutes and then left Peter alone with Mrs. Boardman. She had little chance of lasting the night. It seemed natural for Peter to be alone with her.

Peter thought for awhile, searching his mind for an answer. He was looking for something to say to the others. There had been too much death; it hung over them like a cape. Suddenly he found himself on his knees beside the window gazing into the night sky. Prayer came to him as easily as it had ever come. Peter lost track of time and did not realize that he had been before the window for more than an hour. When he arose, he stopped and made the sign of the cross on the dying woman's forehead and left for his own room. He fell into a deep sleep.

He awoke to the sound of voices coming from Mrs. Boardman's room. He thought he heard her voice. After dressing, Peter made his way down the hall. Mrs. Boardman was sitting upright in bed, very indignant about being allowed to sleep so late. She looked as healthy as anyone else in the room. Peter stood in the doorway for a moment, his eyes filled with tears. His wife walked back to the bedroom with him.

As she paused to kiss him, she said, "My dear, He is very much with us."

As the news of the miracle spread throughout the community, the effect was that of renewed hope for the survivors. Peter spoke to a full church that Sunday, and it was to continue. The cold could not dim the joy within him, and the others felt his hope.

The weather did not appreciably change, although the calendar indicated early summer. The snow still covered the fields, and the river ice held firm. For the children, there would be ice skating all summer.

Warren and Lynn were married by Peter at the farm, with the group and a few of Mrs. Boardman's friends joining in the celebration and reception in the farm kitchen. Later, they left the couple alone by the stove. A bowl of hot rum punch simmered on the top. Lynn stared into the glowing embers, visible on the stove grate.

"War," she spoke, "we never would have been together like this if it hadn't been for Solar III. Funny, I don't mind thinking ahead now. Maybe there is a future somewhere."

"There must be," Warren answered. "The world can't just come to an end like this. We'll find a way to keep going." They watched the fire die down and then went upstairs. For that night, the rest of the world was set aside.

The loss of the summer growing season placed a finite limit on the available food supply. Indeed, for the Vermont survivors, the next winter would be their last. Food could be rationed to a point, but beyond that limit one must have the will to survive. If only there were some indication of a return to normal temperatures, but no such indications were forthcoming.

The task fell to Peter and Bumper to inventory the remaining food stores and to establish rations for one more year. Strange, being able to calculate your life's limit on earth, though beyond the next year what would be the use? Within a year, as they well understood, much could change.

Peter spent considerable time in trying to understand their state. He had not given up hope, but rather wanted a rationale that he could relate to the others. That was what was missing: a rationale, some kind of answer. He had been walking toward the church. Engrossed as he was in his thoughts, he did not notice the man coming toward him.

The stranger stopped about ten feet from Peter and spoke. "You are Peter, are you not?"

Peter was not certain if the stranger actually spoke to him or if he seemed to almost think the conversation in his mind.

He finally returned the greeting. "Yes, I am Peter. Are you going down to the village?"

The stranger did not respond, but joined Peter.

"Where are you from?" asked Peter, trying to establish some informal conversation. The stranger did not answer, but turned and stared at Peter. He was dressed in what appeared to be a body-fitting sweat suit, all gray in color so as to be almost invisible against the snow. But it was his eyes that shocked Peter. There were like two camera lenses constantly photographing you. They were round, dark, but not sinister, more unusual than anything. Peter was startled as the stranger spoke again.

"How much food do you have?"

Peter replied, "About a year's supply if we are careful."

They were approaching the small village church now, and as Peter stopped, the stranger spoke again.

"It will be enough for all of you."

Peter looked back as he started up the church steps, but the stranger had disappeared. There was a small pool of melted snow where he had been standing, and as Peter looked back over his tracks he noticed that the stranger had left none. Peter entered the church. It was cold and dark with most of the windows shuttered. He sat for a while trying to determine if he had been with a person or some sort of a spirit. Yet, the stranger was real in a weird sort of a way. He kept seeing that oval face with those piercing camera-like circular eyes—eyes that entered the innermost depths of your mind and knew everything.

Peter returned to the farm, retracing his footsteps. The stranger had left none. He decided to speak only to his wife about the incident for the moment. He didn't know how to explain it to the others. There had to have been some sort of a being back there with him, and the stranger had seemed to be giving him a message of assurance, but of what? There had to be an explanation for the incident; people just didn't come and go as this stranger had done. In the coming weeks, he would dwell on the stranger's words—nothing in their lives indicated anything but eventual death by starvation and the ever-present cold.

The coming of Warren and Lynn's baby took his mind away from the mysterious meeting. Peter was aware that the conception preceded the marriage, but it was not his way to speak of it. Instead, Peter urged that some of his rations be given to Lynn so that her health would be maintained. If only that child would have a chance to live.

John did most of the firewood hauling and brought the daily food rations in each day from the potato cellars. Wood was one item in plentiful supply. The cold had killed a number of the trees in the woods, and as long as one had the strength to cut and split the logs, a warm farmhouse was assured. He was hauling more than they used because the team would have to be slaughtered in the fall and then all the wood would have to be carried by hand. The thought made him hurry the team for an extra load.

This time John went over the ridge to the back woods, saving the trees closer to the farmhouse for later cutting. Without the team and sled, hauling distance would mean a lot. He pulled the horses up and set out on foot to look for downed timber. Beyond the woods lay the orchard. In better times, it was a beautiful place, first with the spring blossoms and later the smell of rich apples during harvest. The team liked the orchard. They were always allowed to graze on windfalls. Today the trees were barren, probably dead by now, John thought.

As he stood in the orchard, sadness came over him; all that was once so alive and beautiful was lost. John so wanted to show Sherri the farm as it should be in its beauty. This had been his entire life.

To his left on the slope John's eye caught a slight movement and change of color; something or someone was moving near one of the apple trees. He walked cautiously toward it, and the object before him stopped John cold in his tracks. One tree was in full bloom, the grass underneath green and lush. As he watched, the tree progressed in growth through summer, and within minutes the branches were heavy with fruit. John stood speechless for a moment, then picked as many apples as he could and ran back for the team. Returning, he shook some apples down on the ground for the horses and filled the sleigh with as many more as he could reach. Turning the team in spite of their reluctance to leave, John headed back to the house as fast as he could urge the team.

Running inside, he yelled, "Sher, Mom, come quick!"

The group assembled on the porch, and for a moment nothing was said. Finally Bumper pointed to the sleigh load of fruit.

"Where in heaven's name did you get *those*?"

"A tree," John exclaimed. "A tree in the orchard—it's full of fruit. I picked all that I could carry. Come on and see."

They all put on their outdoor clothes and followed John back over the ridge to the orchard. Where the sleigh tracks ended stood the tree, only now it was like all the others, barren with a blanket of snow on the ground underneath.

"But I just picked them!" John stammered to the others. "See?" He pulled one from his coat pocket.

"We don't doubt your word, John," Peter replied. "It is only that we do not understand."

Returning to the farm, they unloaded the sleigh and packed the apples safely away from the cold in the potato cellar. That night the farm smelled of fresh apple pie, cooked in Mrs. Boardman's best tradition.

After the meal, Peter decided that he should tell them about his visit with the stranger. That and the tree incident were somehow related. Warren was a little upset with Peter's not having told them immediately.

"Peter, anything which might help us should be known to us at once. It's not fair to keep something like this secret."

"I'm sorry," was all that Peter could add. He agreed with Warren's critique. Peter continued his discussion. "We have always considered this disaster an act of God, or some natural occurrence, but as some of the villagers are convinced, all of this may be some sort of a takeover of our planet by another intelligent species. That stranger I saw may have been one of them. He was able to melt the snow around him like the tree outside, and perhaps these people can turn heat on and off at their will. Or maybe they have some shield surrounding earth to control the sun's energy we receive."

"But why would they want to kill most of us?" asked Warren

"Would you want this planet in its present state?" replied Peter. "Look at us. Everyone had been fighting in some part of the world, and half of the world could not grow enough food to stay alive. Killing most of the people off might be an easy way to get rid of some excess baggage before they arrive. I think the most important thing for all of us is to believe in something that will bring all of this to an end. I believe in a God, but if God is universal, He may be universal on other planets. The stranger I saw was far advanced from any being on this earth, I am certain, but I cannot call him nonhuman. For those in the village, I have a duty to help them keep their faith, if only to perhaps have them live through whatever this thing is."

Peter at least felt better for having told the group of his experience, and it made him feel better about having to give the church service that Sunday.

There were those who did not believe in Peter's convictions. Some in the village were convinced that Solar III and all its related events were the result of visitors from outer space. Indeed, if some life form wished to take control of earth, the time was now. Those who were left certainly could offer little resistance, particularly if a superior race were involved. There had been strange events and possibly visits in the past. Some believed this could be the final chapter.

Peter himself could understand the logic of both arguments. If his belief was to prevail, he would have to support his position. He had spent most of the week in thought and prayer following the "apple miracle," but as Sunday morning dawned, he was no closer to an answer than that night with the group at the farm. Peter had put together a sermon of sorts. He was not pleased with the content, but nonetheless he carried it to the service that Sunday.

Facing the congregation, Peter opened his notes. As he looked at the contents, they blurred. Yet he began with his text: "The meek shall inherit the earth." He couldn't remember afterwards what he had said, but others told him that his message gave them an answer. Perhaps, just perhaps, those left on earth had one thing in common. They were not the ones with power and wealth; they were men of the earth—farmers, laborers, and children. Again Peter did not fully understand. Not everyone agreed with his message, but he had strengthened the faith of many, including his own.

There was division and considerable discussion as to the ultimate fate of those left on earth. The outer space theory was popular in that it was logical and earth in the past had been visited by others—at least some believed the visits to be real. A super-intelligent power could easily regulate the sun's energy received by earth and reduce the population to some suitable level. For those who survived, what would it be? Servitude? Slavery? No one would hazard a guess.

19.
Coming

Time was no longer measured by the seasons, for there were none, but instead by the amount of food remaining, and for Warren and Lynn by the coming birth of their child. There was some resentment in the village about another mouth to feed, but Peter had argued that with all the death in the world, a promise of new life was good. He had talked to Warren and Lynn, and though he sensed some problem between them over the expected birth, he did not feel it his right to probe into the matter.

Though Warren was convinced he was not the father of the child, he had kept the thoughts to himself. Warren had a deep love for Lynn. He had known one marriage without it, and was not going to be responsible for another similar relationship. There had to be an answer other than her being with another man at Stongsfjörd.

The holidays usually filled with tourists, parades, and parties passed almost unnoticed. Fourth of July, Labor Day, and the usual start of school turned into autumn with the ground snow-covered and extra wood for the stoves piled in rows beside the homes.

Their radio communication with the outside world kept the group aware of the grim reality that their numbers were dwindling. Each time a station contact was lost, a few more brave souls passed on. Many were reluctant to tell of their hardships. They were almost embarrassed to admit defeat. In fact, many said nothing until the end; they simply signed off. The next call attempt would result in silence. Bumper often wondered just how many were left now—a few thousand in each country possibly, no more than that.

Mary Boardman had saved the last goose for the Thanksgiving dinner. She had always felt that the holiday was a special one, and hardship or not, she would do her best to prepare a feast. For days prior to the event, the farmhouse smelled of days gone by—pies, stuffing, and finally the roasting bird.

Peter was about to say the grace as they sat beside the table when the steeple bell in the village began to peal. Its ring was sharp and clear in the cold. The group listened for a moment in silence. Peter was the first to speak.

"Charlie, you, Bumper, and I best go down to see what's up. The rest of you start eating. Don't know how long we'll be."

They dressed against the cold and made their way through the snow to the village.

When they arrived, it seemed that most of the villagers had gathered around and within the church. The building was there as before, but now it appeared as it would on a warm summer day. All evidence of snow was melted from the roof and steeple, with the immediate area surrounding the building also completely free of snow and ice. The crowd was quiet, with many shedding jackets and scarves. As they entered the church, Peter noticed that the interior was almost too warm for comfort, with many sitting in the pews with nothing more than summer wear on. Eventually, most of the residents entered and sat quietly, just enjoying the first feeling of warmth in many months. Some of the men even opened the windows, and a warm breeze swept the interior. Peter walked to the front of the church with the idea of saying something until he saw the figure high in the choir loft at the rear of the church. It was his stranger of a few days ago, and Peter could not help but stare into those camera-seeing eyes. The stranger slowly moved his head back and forth, as if to scan the congregation like a video camera filming the interior. If others saw the stranger, they did not show concern.

Peter viewed the congregation for a moment, and when he looked up again the stranger was gone. Almost on cue the congregation rose and quietly walked out of the building into the snow that was now starting to fall on the front steps. They were still quiet, with some actually smiling, and Peter knew that the stranger had somehow communicated with them as he had done on their encounter. That night for the first time he heard laughter and voices coming from the village.

Peter stayed up past midnight listening, watching, and then slipped outside to be alone. The sky was brilliant, and for once the fog had lifted. He looked to the stars. Perhaps there was an answer up there on some far-off planet. Soon, it would be Christmas.

December was bitter cold. From the radio contacts, the effect was worldwide. Few had been as fortunate as the group on Thanksgiving. Indeed, Charlie had cautioned against spreading the word of the miracle; it might attract food robbers—if, indeed, any survived.

His caution was not necessary. Peter had no way of knowing that there were fewer than ten thousand people alive in the United States. All were in the rural areas. Save for a few rats feeding on the flesh of the unburied, America's cities were empty. It was better Peter didn't know. Faith can be tried to the breaking point.

Christmas preparations were divided between a meager attempt to celebrate the holiday with decorations and small gifts, and concern for Lynn, who was due to deliver her child. Sara and Mary had rehearsed their roles as midwives. Beyond the simple preparations available at the farmhouse, there was nothing else to deal with. If problems arose, there was no assurance Lynn or the child could be saved. Warren was nervous, irritable, and just plain afraid. He stayed close to Lynn. Often the couple would just sit in silence, holding hands and staring out the window at the endless expanse of snow.

Warren knew that he could not survive if Lynn died. If he lost her, he would lose his will to fight the damnable cold. For whatever time his child lived, they could share the love and joy jointly. Beyond that, he could only hope.

The villagers met just before Christmas to again discuss the animal slaughter. Without feed, they decided to keep only enough stock for breeding and use the others for food. There was no discussion about next winter. For the village, there would be none; starvation would claim them. It was agreed among the men to wait until after Christmas to start the butchering. Somehow, killing was not appropriate to the season, even in these times.

The wind picked up all day Christmas Eve. By evening the howl of the storm shook the farmhouse. Charlie and Gus had been in the village listening to the radio. A few contacts attempted to sing carols, then each had wished a "Merry Christmas" and signed off. No mention was made of their situations, for on this, and Christmas day, the realities of death would not be discussed.

Peter had led a service in the village earlier in the day. The storm cut attendance to a few hardy souls. He had asked them to remember the birth and the message of hope to the world almost two thousand years ago.

"Do not lose that hope," Peter had asked them. He had also reminded them of the Thanksgiving miracle—they were not alone. Someone cared.

"Mrs. Boardman, you'd better come up." It was Sara calling from Lynn's room. As Mary left the living room, Peter put his hand on Warren's shoulder.

"I think the time has come."

They tried to sing carols, talk, and take turns getting wood for the stove. Mary wanted hot water. The pots steamed on the stove top, fogging the windows.

Peter finally told the man, "Get some sleep; I'll tend the fires." Reluctantly they left him alone. Peter dozed off and on. He would awake, check the water, feed the stove with firewood, and fall asleep.

He couldn't remember how long he'd been asleep in the chair when something woke him. He was hot, actually sweating, and his first thought was that he had overstocked the stove. Peter staggered over to the stove and opened the fire door. The coals were cold on the grate.

Then he heard it; the sound of water running off the roof. The snow was melting from the heat.

Sara's voice brought him back fully awake.

"Daddy!" she was crying from upstairs. "Come up here."

"I'm on my way." Peter responded, shedding his blanket as he ascended to the bedroom. Warren was sitting beside Lynn, and they both smiled faintly as he entered. She was holding the newborn wrapped in what seemed to be an endless number of blankets, yet the room was hot to the point of being uncomfortable.

Lynn was the first to speak. "Would you like to see our son?" Her voice was quiet, yet strong, and she appeared to have come through the birthing without difficulty.

Peter went to her side and slowly removed the part of the blanket that covered the baby's face. The features were all there, including those large, round, camera-like eyes and the oval face he had seen twice before. As Peter looked out the bedroom window toward the village, the sky was bright blue and the sun was shining. He was beginning to understand it all.

Below, in the valley, some of the villagers were slowly walking up the lane toward the farm. They were singing—they knew, the world knew, that the end had come, and the beginning.

WAR KIDS 1941–1945
WWII Through the Eyes of Children
Lloyd Hornbostel

The 50th anniversary of the peace that ended World War II has inspired the publication of many new books that describe virtually every aspect of that conflict. But often obscured by the grand deeds of generals and armies are the very people for whom the war was fought—our children.

War Kids 1941-1945 succeeds in evoking both the humor and the pathos of children in such a situation. Many of the stories relate uproarious incidents arising from the shenanigans of unsupervised children with too much time of their hands, but all are tinged with the ever-present spectre of tragedy.

Sometimes bittersweet, frequently raucous, Lloyd Hornbostel's writing bristles with a dry, Midwestern wit and vivid descriptions of rural life. *War Kids* is a book that will stir the emotions and memories of anyone living during that period. At the same time, it is an intimate memorial to the innovative, indomitable spirit of youth.

1–880090–27–9, 5½ x 8½, softcover, 128 pgs., $10.95
Please include $3.00 postage and handling for first book, 50¢ for each additional copy.

For other titles of related interest, write for our free catalog.
Send your request to:

Galde Press, Inc.
PO Box 460
Lakeville, Minnesota 55044

Credit card orders call **1–800–777–3454**